THE *ERSATZ*
&
THE TALISMAN

TWO TALES OF AN UNCERTAIN FUTURE

by

CHARLES NUETZEL

The Borgo Press
An Imprint of Wildside Press

MMVII

FIRST EDITION

CONTENTS

INTRODUCTION

The Ersatz was originally published as a paperback novel under the title, *Lovers: 2075*, and then later in a slightly improved version as part of *Images of Tomorrow*, a collection published by Powell Publications in 1969.

Now I offer it to a new set of twenty-first-century readers in this new updating of the original text.

Ersatzes exist in a world where universal peace, population control and boredom drove people to the edge of violence. The *Ersatz* was the ideal solution to such social rage!

Angry at your boss—take it out on your *ersatz*. That's what they are for!

Nagged by your wife—whack your *ersatz* instead of her!

Have a husband who is cheating on you—blow your *ersatz*'s head off!

That's what they were made for! And there was an endless supply of these android creatures! Even in an over-populated world. *Ersatzes* could be recycled! Mindless, soulless inventions of human science, they were the ultimate solution to man's problems.

Only the National Organization FREE spoke to change things. FREE = For Rising *Ersatz* Equality!

Only FREE was mad enough to believe that *ersatzes* might offer much more to its masters than simply an outlet for its violent nature.

It was a losing cause, until....

Benny arrived!

"The Talisman" is a new and original story that I found in my files—lost until now. If I remember right, it came out of my dislike of door-to-door salesmen, but then it quickly became something totally different. It was written some years ago and simply filed away. I gave it to my friendly editor, Heidi Garrett, who loved it and encouraged me to put it with *The Ersatz*. And so it is here presented.

—Charles Nuetzel
Thousand Oaks, California
July 2006

THE *ERSATZ*

FOREWORD

The legends and myths that developed around the Revolution, and how it all began for Jean, are filled with fairy tales, distortions and simply bad reporting. It is in an effort to regain some sanity about the early beginnings, the events which were considered vital in the historical overthrow of the old government, that this book is being offered. What follows is the earliest surviving text that tells of how the Original Bonding formed, which would in later years plant the seeds to set the world free! The author is unknown, but all historians agree that herein is a realistic portrayal of events as they actually must have happened. Dramatized in "fictional" form, they ring with the hard truth of a soundly based news story. Most of all it was written during her lifetime.

CHAPTER ONE

He had been hiding and walking for most of the night in a blind terror, in a frantic horror that any moment the Social Police would step out of some dark corner and take him to the Chemical Lab for destruction. But no hand had reached from the black of night or the secret shadows which loomed like dark, foreboding arms attempting to grab at him. No Civilian teen-age gang had trapped him at a street corner to run a shiv across his guts or beat him senseless. For nobody killed another human being in the twenty-first Century. And that's what they thought he was.

But he was an *ersatz,* which meant that he didn't have any rights. He was there for the use of anyone who wanted his services, which included his meek acceptance to being beaten to death with clubs or fists, or sliced by razor sharp knives. *They* could even drop him into deep space so that his life would explode away.

So, he was running. He didn't know how long he would remain free, because the Social Police would find him—today, tomorrow or the next week. It didn't really matter. But there was that in him that cried for freedom, no matter how short it might be. For a little while he would have this freedom that human beings enjoyed from their birth. Those people born of women who didn't consider *him* human; they didn't consider an *ersatz* human—yet he couldn't help believing himself as human as the others. What really made him so different? Just because he had been born in a chemical vat? Did that mean he didn't have emotions or the will to live and the fear of dying and of pain? He had the desire to love and hate, to be loved and hated because he was an individual personality; to feel the joys and the bitter sorrows of life—but equal to those of the other men. Weren't those the qualities that made men human?

It was morning now, the red fire of the hot sun was breaking down over the city, bringing its warm light to melt the cold darkness and the horrible chill of death that had iced fear through him during the night hours.

He was walking down one of the lonely morning streets. His eyes took in the low, flat homes; watched the men and women through the large windows beginning to awaken to the day and the activities that would keep the civilized world producing the merchandise which was to be consumed with a hungry, desperate anxiety, as if they couldn't use enough bad cablevisions or enough bad washing machines or enough bad cars, which obediently broke down after six months of frantic use to be replaced quickly by new bad merchandise. This was the world of senseless insanity where people went about doing the same things each day in order to keep their minds occupied and off the world problems of population control and wonderful glorious peace. No more religious wars to bring terror into the minds of men of different faiths. Such madness was controlled, channeled. This was a world where *ersatzes* were killed to release simple frustrations. A man's wife didn't make love to him that evening; a woman's cooking didn't come out as she had expected! Or a Video didn't satisfy the frustrated viewer. Any reason from unreturned love to the fact that a child woke up in the morning with a slight cold, was cause enough to kill one of his kind.

Ersatzes came cheap!

There was the problem of over-crowding the world, solved by rigid birth control laws. *Ersatzes* were a necessary evil, to keep a tight rein on sanity. Couples couldn't have more than one child, and then only with government permission. There weren't enough challenging jobs for everybody and most people were bored and frustrated by the crowded living conditions. Only the rich could afford small homes like these now around Jim.

If your boss gave you a bad time it was easy to take it out on your *ersatz*. Kill the *ersatz* or beat it senseless—after all, that's what they were invented for. Release your angers and hates and disgusts and the personal horrors which plague you, give them all to your *ersatz*—and become a better member of society! They said this was morally right. Don't put the problems on society but on the *ersatz*!

That was the Law! Because crime was not permitted, violence against another human being was not permitted; anger against another human being was not allowed. Hate was not permitted. Experience those feelings? Well. Take it out on your *ersatz*! *"That's what they are for!"*

Didn't they know or care that an *ersatz* had feelings; that they wanted the same things that their human inventors wanted, and needed? Didn't they realize that an *ersatz* was much like themselves? After all, the *ersatzes* had been made in the image and likeness of their creator. In each and every way!

"Good morning, sir," a man greeted, as he passed on the sidewalk.

He nodded and smiled back. They couldn't tell an *ersatz* from one of them, unless they looked at the number tattooed on the *ersatz*'s arm. Wasn't that proof that he wasn't any different? He was number B-7978684208T03—but his owner called him Benny. Nobody could see that number as long as he wore the forbidden human clothing. All *ersatzes* wore nothing but g-strings made of gray silk; that was their mark of distinction; their identity. Their public brand!

He wondered where he would go, what he would do. As long as he kept moving, everything would be okay, because everybody would believe he was going somewhere important like other humans. They might think he was going to work. It wouldn't occur to them he was just aimlessly wandering, keeping on the move, trying to escape detection. They wouldn't think he was a runaway *ersatz*, trying to find freedom and trying desperately to keep his life.

Last night his owner, Mr. John Smithington Adams, had come home angered with his boring and uncreative job. He was a file clerk for the Great Eastern Insurance Company. Mr. Adams was a stupid little man, who couldn't be held responsible for anything other than filing on a computer. He had been filing for thirty of his fifty-five years of life.

He really never knew what he was filing, or where it went, but merely click-click-clicked all day on the computer. That was his job, assignment. He suspected, as many others in his social status, that the job was a make-work activity. But that didn't matter. It was required of him. He hated it! His wife was drunk and unconscious in her bedroom when he got home, and Mr. Adams had come to Benny. Something bad had happened that day at the office; but Benny had no way of knowing what had triggered his master; all that mattered was the fact that this time it had felt different. The open look of hate, anguish and violence which was generated in his insanely pinched face had left little doubt in Benny's mind that this surely would be the end for B-7978684208T03. Benny had always wondered what he would do at this moment of decision, which was sure to come; this moment of facing death, helpless to defend himself. He had stood there quietly waiting as Mr. Adams picked up a metal chair and moved toward him. Benny had thought he could just stand there and let the man kill him. The frantic fear which came to him at that moment generated only one thought: *Run, run, don't stand there and let this foolish' little man kill you!*

And he had run, pushing Adams to one side and rushing past the man, out of the room, down the hall and then out of the house. After the first panic ebbed away he went back to the house, which was now empty. He guessed that Adams had gone to the Robo Police Station to report his escape. Benny quickly got some clothes, which were just a little too small for him, from the closet, and dressed. Then he rushed out of the house and disappeared into the shadows, until he was finally out of the immediate district of his owner's shabby little home.

Benny's attention shifted to the present.

A young girl, not over seven, was jumping rope on the sidewalk ahead of him. She looked in his direction and smiled warmly, and as he stepped up to her:

"Hello, Mister."

It was the way that she said it. So much sunshine was bursting inside her. She didn't have any way of releasing it except through her words and voice. She was a happy little face, grinning toothily up with such vital friendship that he found himself standing and staring down at her, suddenly feeling good about himself and life. Her cheeks were pink and puffed and her eyes squinted in the bright smile. There was something about her that he hadn't seen in many human children. Most children were angrily selfish, demanding, cruel and hateful. But this little girl expressed only an open bubbling love.

"What are you looking at, Mister?" she asked, suddenly serious, her lips closing over her little white teeth.

Benny realized he had been staring at her for a long time. He smiled and was rewarded by the return of her happy grin.

"Just at you, little girl," he answered carefully, hoping he sounded like any other human.

"Why?" she asked childishly, throwing her rope under her legs and jumping over it. The freshly ironed, yellow skirt flew up in the air.

"You looked so happy. Is this some special day for you?"

"Oh, yes. It's *very* special. Today we get my

first *ersatz*. Today is my birthday. I'm seven. Old enough to have my own *ersatz*. I'll love him so very much. We can play and do all sorts of things together!" Her face was shaded in soft sadness. Then she smiled again. "Can you play with me?"

"I—I don't know," he told her, suddenly confused. Oddly he found himself wanting to stay with her There was a wonderful sense of love in her eyes, an eagerness which radiated from her with such open honesty that he wanted to take her into his arms and hold her tightly to him, run his fingers through her soft blonde hair. He wanted to comfort and protect her. It was a strange emotion to him. One that he had never felt for any human being before. It defied logic. Then caution stopped him.

"I'm sorry, I have to go. You know how it is with adults. We have to keep busy. Going, going. We have to keep doing things. If we don't keep busy and do things we won't have all the nice things in our homes."

"You have a little girl like me?"

"No. I have no little girl."

"Oh," she sighed. For a moment she was thoughtful and then said: "I like you."

He stood there, nervously, not knowing what to do or what to say. Then sighing, he forced a smile.

"Thank you—I better get going." Then without another word he started down the sidewalk away from the little girl.

The morning traffic was already beginning to get heavy and when he came to the end of the block he had to wait for several moments before he could cross the street. He was just stepping onto the far side when the young girl's voice called after him.

"Mister—Mister, wait!"

Benny turned and saw the little girl rushing up to the other side of the street and then, to his horror, saw her start across toward him, unaware of the traffic, blinded to everything but her childish destination.

"Don't! Stay there!" he warned.

But she kept coming.

A ground car was speeding at her, unable to stop in time.

Benny sprang toward her, frantically trying to reach the little girl before the racing death. His *ersatz* muscles shot him forward much faster than any human could have ever covered the distance. He was sweeping her into his arms, still leaping forward, when the terrible impact of the car skidded against his legs. Frantically he thrust the girl out of danger, dragging himself across the street. He was hurt, but wasn't damaged beyond repair, for his synflesh was stronger than human flesh and his steel bones were stronger than human bones. He reached the sidewalk just before the pain in his crippled legs ripped at his brain-centers with such force that consciousness numbed to blackness. Benny's last thought was that freedom was over, his escape a failure! He had given it away by saving the little girl. But even then, he realized in a vague numbness just before awareness completely slipped, it had been well worth it. He had proven that even an *ersatz* could be brave and self-sacrificing. The little girl stumbled to her feet, dazed, stunned, looking down at the man who had just saved her life. For a moment, anguished tears blinded her and she wanted to die. *He had been such a nice man,* she thought, agonized.

"Are you all right?" a man's voice asked. "That guy moved as fast as an *ersatz*! I never saw such a thing'." a matronly woman's voice cried in amazement.

"Is it the girl's father?" another voice wanted to know.

The matronly woman said: "Of course it is. Who else would risk their life for a little girl?"

"No. No!" the little girl cried, opening her eyes and looking at the surrounding people. "He's just a nice man.

"I do declare," the matronly woman exclaimed, "hear that! Somebody risking their life for a little girl!"

"That's unheard of. He must be a very stupid or strange person," the tall man said, awed.

"Is he alive?" the woman wanted to know.

The man stooped over and looked at Benny, placing a thick hand over his heart. "My God! How in the world could he live through such a thing?"

A policeman came up, looked at the crowd. "What's happened here?"

"This man saved this girl's life!" the woman said, stoutly. "A brave man.

"How'd it happen?" the officer demanded in a coldly authoritative voice.

"The little girl just rushed across the street toward him, shouting," the matronly woman explained. "He turned and yelled something to her and then rushed and whipped the poor little darling into his arms just in time to save her life."

The police officer leaned down and examined Benny. "He looks seriously hurt. But the medicos can fix that. I'll call—you see to it he's not moved. Little girl, stay here, 'cause I have to talk to you." The officer rushed off and then in a few minutes returned.

There was a large crowd around Benny now and the officer had to push through it. He stopped before the little girl and said: "I've got to ask you some questions. What's your name, little girl?"

"Jeannie Brown.

"Where do you live?"

"Down the street. 709—that way." She pointed to her home. "I was playing when this nice man came along. We got to talking. He walked away and I just wanted to tell him to come by again and talk to me I didn't mean for him to get hurt or anything like that."

"It's quite all right. He'll be okay. The medicos will fix his legs. Nothing to worry about little girl," the officer assured her, gently patting Jeannie's blonde head.

Just then the sound of a high-pitched siren broke the city noises; the high frequency bringing all the automatically controlled cars to a stop and moving them to the side of the road. Then as an ambulance pulled up to the corner, the siren choked out of existence, and the traffic continued on as normal. Two men in tight fitting white suits rushed from the ambulance and through the crowd. One of them, carrying a small black bag, stooped down over the silent form on the street and pulled aside the outer jacket, examining his chest. For a moment he puzzled over Benny with instruments and then angrily stood, savagely turning to the police officer.

"What's the meaning of this?" he demanded, his

eyes becoming bright with indignation.

"What do you mean?"

"This is an *ersatz!*"

There was a stunned silence which blanketed over the crowd as the announcement shattered the air. For a moment they stood there and then one by one cringed away, moving down the street, going their different directions as if they had been told the Devil himself were lying on the street.

"You must be fooling!" the policeman cried, alarmed. "That's impossible. He saved the life of this little girl. *Ersatzes* don't do such things! It's unheard of."

The medico stared blankly at the officer and then gulped a hard lump at his throat. Beads of sweat formed on his forehead and then his eyes darted to Benny and then slowly moved back to the officer. "There must be something wrong here."

"There were eye-witnesses. This is the little girl he saved!" The officer pointed to Jeannie Brown who was looking innocently and happily at the medico..

"It's true, Medico," she cried excitedly "Isn't it wonderful?" Then a thought occurred to her. "Oh, this *is* wonderful! Now I can have him for my own. I can have him to play with. He can play hop-scotch with me. He can-"

"Wait, little girl. He belongs to somebody. And he'll have to be returned," the police officer told her. "Once I get his number we'll discover who he belongs to—and then..." The man shrugged, patting the little girl on the head.

"But this is my birthday. And I'm seven. I'm old enough to have an *ersatz*. And I want *this* one!" she insisted, on the verge of tears.

The Medico and the Officer exchanged glances and then the policeman took hold of the little girl's hand. "Well, anyway—we have to take you home, so that your mother won't be worried about you. Then I'll come back and make my report." The last sentence was directed at the Medico who sighed a breath of relief.

Nobody wanted the responsibility of anything out of the ordinary. Not in the world of the twenty-first century.

CHAPTER TWO

Edmund Canfield was in his office, at the *National Star,* when the report came in. It came over the CMS—the Cell Media Service! As he watched the information feeding into the computer, Edmund felt a wave of excitement and then depression.

Ken Merrill came storming into his office a moment later.

"See the flash?" Ken cried, running thick fingers across a bald head. His red, puffy features were wide with amazement, making his eyes seem to pop from their sockets.

"I see it," Edmund said, feeling a tightness at the center of his stomach. He also saw what was coming.

"I want you to cover it!" Ken announced.

"Look...that's something I want to talk to you about."

"What's there to talk about?" Ken frowned, plunging his large hands onto the shiny slick surface of the desk. He leaned over, on his arms, glaring at Edmond.

"You know Claire...well, she hit the roof like a sputtering rocket last night because of my last editorial about the *ersatzes*. I made a promise to her about not doing anything more on the-"

"What!...the...hell?" Ken exploded, accenting each word as if it were an individual rocket shooting off to Mars.

"Look, do me a favor—we've been buddies for years—get me off the hook about this thing. No more *ersatz* stories. I have enough problems about that with Claire. She's a nut on the subject."

"Look, Ed, that's too bad. You're the best re-porter we have so good you get that editorial slot...you know the subject—and you can get into places others can't. *Especially* because of your con-nection with Claire!"

The two stared at each other for a long time be-fore either said anything.

From the hard look in Ken's eyes, Edmund knew it was useless to argue. The very air seemed to crackle with the energy bursting between them.

Finally Edmund sighed and then said: "Look, do this much: no by-lines. Just straight report-ing...okay?"

"That serious? On a class story like this? Like the class story I expect you to write? The whole works, Ed! I want details. Everything you know. All the ins and all the outs."

"I'll use a pen-name—how's that?"

"Suit yourself. But give me the story. The whole works. That's what I demand!"

"What kind of slant?"

"Any kind of slant which will fire up the public. No mushy stuff. Be tough, cut hard give them what they want!" With that Ken Merrill snapped around and jerked out of the office.

Edmund sat there, leaning against the padded steel chair, looking up at the ceiling, trying to fight the nervous grind which was churning in his stomach. He felt like a bastard. His promise to Claire had been an honest one. He'd never really lied to her. That was one thing they'd had between them from the very beginning; honesty. Once the lies started, it could be difficult to stop them.

* * * * * * *

Last night it had started when they arrived at his apartment. Edmund had tried to sidetrack Claire from an argument over the *ersatzes* and the article he had written for the Telenews that afternoon. His method had simply been to pull her into his arms, making the first pass that would lead them to more interesting destination.

But she had pushed him away.

"I don't care," she announced with a thin edge of anger in her voice, "how many times you kiss me—that won't change my mind. That editorial you did was crap!"

Her fists slammed to her waist as dark green eyes challenged his. Claire Richards looked beautiful when she was miffed. Her creamy yellow dress clung to every delicious curve of her lovely body.

"Do we *have* to go into it again?" Edmund demanded in desperation. Already they had covered the subject, since he had picked her up for dinner, at least half a dozen times. "It is all just part of my job!"

"You *don't* have to like it so damned much!" Claire cried pacing the small living room. "You know how I feel!"

"I didn't bring you up here to fight!" Edmund

announced a little angrily.

"Who's fighting? It...is just that I *really* care!"

"Look. Claire, I only expressed the general opinion of the public. *Ersatzes* are *not* human and no matter how much you people try to say differently you're all wet!" he announced, walking across the ultra-modern apartment to the wall-bar panel. He pressed a button. then dialed the combination for a Stellar Cocktail and a Rocket Flame.

A moment later a slot opened in the wall-panel and two glasses slid slowly out of the robo-tray which offered the drinks.

"Here, have a drink and let's get it over with." He handed Claire the Rocket Flame, a combination of gin, rum and fruit juices. "Now your claim is that an *ersatz* is something more than synflesh and metal, that they are semi-human, that they *think* and have *emotions*...that's a lot of comet dust and you know it! Of all people you *should* know it working for *Ersatz, Inc.* And should be pushing for status quo! And—"

"Eddy, they're *programmed* to have all the reactions that humans do. They have 'personalities,' they have memory banks, and they have electro nervous systems, so that they *do* react like humans. That's the whole idea! The *ersatz* is the substitute human—the '*ersatz*' on which hate, violence murder—all the human emotions—can be let out on. But what if an *ersatz* proved itself to be more human than we think?"

"That's silly and you know it."

"But, just think. *Ersatzes* might serve a far grander purpose as a partner in the exploration of space, say ... better than robots, since they could react and function on a human level?"

"Next thing you'll say they should be love-mates!" he laughed.

"Don't be surprised it that could very well come about—if the public demanded it!" she murmured, half to herself.

"Oh, come on, that's fantasyland!"

"No way! There's unlimited possibilities! Not that I'm in any way promoting *ersatz* call girls! There's better things they could do…far better than their present limited function!" she announced, quiet seriously.

"Enough!" Edmund placed an arm around her body. He drew her close and kissed her lips.

For a moment they stood there, aware of nothing other than the nearness of each other.

Edmund had never known a woman like Claire, he had never been in love before. He wondered how long it would last.

As Claire pushed away from him, her cheeks were flushed, her breath heavy

"I love you. you slob!" she laughed. "Why the hell can't you see things my way?"

"Do I have to?"

"No…but be would nice!"

"I didn't invited you up here to argue about those damned *ersatzes*." He followed her across the room toward the bedroom.

"Well, at least you don't own one. That's a credit to you!"

"I'm just not the violent type. And believe me it took a lot of pull!" he laughed as the door closed behind him. He reached for the bed-switch on the wall.

27

The lights had turned on the moment they walked into the room and as his finger touched the bed-switch, the far wall opened down, slid forward and a large king size bed presented itself.

"Put on the ocean scene," Claire requested, settling down on the bed. She undid her hair—which had been done up high on her head. The golden blonde locks fell over her creamy white shoulders.

Edmund turned away, reluctantly. It was hard to be in the same room with Claire without feasting on her beauty every minute.

His fingers flicked another switch and a little dial-box slid out of the wall.

"Let's see—that's D-7 15...and a little music?"

"Of course! Ocean music and romantic violins. 776B." His fingers dialed out the numbers. "It's on VA!"

"Why don't you have it always on Voice Activation?"

"It is, most of the time…"

First the lighting dimmed, then the side wall of the room shimmered and a moment later they were looking at the beautiful Pacific Ocean which stretched out in full color as far as the eye could see. It was like looking through a huge window across a short beach below. Then music swelled into being, soft and romantic.

"I wish we were there!" Claire sighed. "I've never really seen the beach...or the ocean, for that matter. That's the trouble with living in this century—you're boxed in. I read a book, once, about the Second World War during the twentieth century. Things were so different. And the years that followed. They—"

"Claire you're talking too much!" He walked over to the bed and sat down next to her.

"But I was only saying that the living conditions are terrible if you compare them to what they used to be! Look at the way they are! Only the slums and the rich areas are lower than twenty stories high! Then you have the skyscrapers—it's depressing!"

"You making fun of my apartment?" he teased, caressing her neck with the point of his finger.

"Don't!" she murmured happily, twisting her head from side to side. "I didn't mean that. So you have an apartment in the Towers! So what? I have one like it too...but...sometimes I wish..."

"You talk too much!" he laughed, patting her cheek.

They looked at one another for a short time and then Claire shrugged. "Okay—no more conversation!"

How I love her! he thought, sliding down beside Claire.

There was a softness in her eyes, a haunting beautiful expression which expressed deep love and affection.

"Do you think," she asked, "that we'll ever stop arguing?"

"I really don't care!" He reached out and caressed her shoulder.

"You're a beast! You know that?" she murmured contentedly.

"But an up and coming reporter!"

"I thought you said no more talking about—"

He cut the words off by covering her lips with his. The kiss lingered for a moment and then she pulled away.

Edmund reached under the bed, pulled out a small table on which a magnetized cigarette case was waiting. He puffed two cigarettes until they lit up and handed one to Claire.

"Perverting me again. Back a few hundred decades ago..."

"Cancer free, and you know it!"

"Ages ago they were deadly," she laughed. "Now only *you* are deadly!"

He nodded.

"I'll never get over meeting you, Claire," he announced.

They had met some time ago at the National Press Conference, a two-day affair in which all the members of the *National Star* got together, from all over the world, and listened to dull, uninteresting speeches and partied during the evenings. Claire had been there because she was interested in the FREE—The National Organization for Rising *Ersatz* Equality—the president of which was giving a speech pleading for editorial promotion for their cause. Edmund had met her at the cocktail lounge and they began the argument which had raged between them ever since. But that night they'd gone out on the town, dined, danced and ended up in his hotel room. Something had clicked; both physically and emotionally. Edmund had never known a woman with whom he could argue and make love to; and want more.

They were silent for a moment, and then she said: "Really, Eddy, can't you lay off the *ersatz* thing. Just for me?"

"Again?" He sighed, sitting up and looked out the 'window' at the expanse of the make-believe ocean.

"Again…and always!" she promised. "That's what I'm all about. How I am. And you know it. I'm a dedicated, fanatic type of lady—"

"So I've noticed," he laughed, touching her naked thigh. "But dedicated to FREE rather than *Ersatz*, Inc."

"Oh, bosh, and you know it. The company has a lot of FREE thinking people. We see the future and…"

His hand was caressing her shoulder, lips following the fingers along her naked flesh.

"Do you have to do that?"

"What?" he innocently countered.

"Well, you know…that makes me…lose track of my thoughts."

"Intended motive!" he offered.

"You're a nasty man!"

"Always…" He murmured thoughtfully.

"As I was saying, dear…promise me?" She pleaded with her lovely eyes. "Give the *ersatzes* a break…*please!*"

"Always pitching!" he groaned, turning and facing her. His expression was drawn, serious. "I follow orders—I do what the editor tells me."

"Oh, come on, Eddy…"

"Look, if it'll make you feel better, I'll talk to Ken and see if we can tone it down a bit."

Claire's eyes brightened and she fairly leaped upwards into his arms, hugging him.

"I didn't think it would mean *that* much to you. After all, what is *one* small voice?"

"That many less voices!" she announced happily. "It makes me feel I'm doing my part, at least!"

She hugged tightly to him, then her lips reached for his.

She leaned back down on the bed, said: "I love you, Eddy. I don't really want to talk any more...about anything! You certainly didn't bring me here for a long, dull conversation did you?"

"That was my line."

"So we agree on *one* topic. anyway!" she said throatily, just before their lips met.

* * * * * * *

Now in his office, the memory of Claire's young lovely form melting against his own, soften the irritation about her endless arguments over the *ersatzes*. In her arms he could forgive anything. He had never known a woman quite like her. Probably in another generation, another time, they might already be married.

Sighing, Edmund pressed the arm of the chair and the back slowly slid down into a reclining position. He pushed another button and the desk before him opened up, revealing an audio-keyboard with the mike thrusting out toward him.

He sat and thought, tried to clear his mind of the personal relationship between Claire and himself. It was some moments before he started talking:

Headline caption:

"*ERSATZ* SAVES CHILD'S LIFE."

Paragraph:

"An *ersatz* known to his owner as

Benny escaped from his master last night, and during the morning hours was hit by a ground car—"

The computer started humming softly, rapidly recording the words as he spoke them.

"…It is not generally considered normal for an *ersatz* to behave in such a manner. They are programmed, as every school child knows, to respond to their master's wish and desire, regardless of what that might be. The only conclusion to be made is that the *ersatz* Benny is defective and will be returned to the lab for disposal."

End article. Run it on page one. Close.

Edmund stood and the chair folded up into the correct position. The computer clicked on for a moment longer and then slipped back into place inside the desk which closed up to reveal only the shiny metal surface.

* * * * * * *

Edmund stepped out of the ground-cab and then walked up the steps to the large skyscraper in which *Ersatz Inc.* was located. He had called Claire to expect him.

The doors opened as he approached and then he stepped to the elevator tube which took him to the seventy-fifth floor. A few moments later he walked into a neat, orderly white office, in which there was

33

only the necessary amount of furniture; a desk, much like his own, and an extra chair in front of it.

Claire stepped around the desk and came into his arms. "Oh, Eddy, I'm glad to see you. You don't know how hellish it's been since the report about the *ersatz*. Bells are ringing, rockets are flying and—"

His kiss stopped her words in mid-flight. She pressed firmly against him and he felt an immediate reaction to her soft nearness. Her dress was more conservative than the one she'd worn the other evening, but still sensually exciting. The neckline dipped low.

The kiss lingered for a moment and then they stepped away from each other.

Her eyes twinkled up at him. "What's the visit for?"

"What do you think?" Edmund inquired.

"Not about the Benny story—you aren't doing anything on that, are you?" she demanded in a stony voice.

"I'm just asking questions—and giving it to another guy to do the writing."

She frowned for a moment, her lower lip tucked under even white teeth. "What do you want to know, Eddy?"

"What's the story—from the inside?"

Claire walked around her desk and sat down before answering him. She motioned Edmund into the chair opposite her.

As he sat, he pressed his wrist-cell, activating its recorder. He felt like a slob, taking advantage of Claire in this way, but it was his job.

"I looked up the record on 'Benny'. Everybody's calling him Benny, here. Anyway, there's nothing to show that he's different." She smiled knowingly at him. But there was a harsh wall between them which she seemed to feel as strongly as he did.

"And?" Edmund pushed, professionally. He tried to convince himself that he was talking to a stranger—a person to be interviewed, rather than to the woman he loved.

"They're performing another examination on Benny. The last report was that they couldn't find anything defective about him." Her expression changed excitedly. "You see what this means? Do you understand what it'll mean to the whole world?"

"I see it can be a good story for a couple of days—that's all I know," he said, carefully.

"Oh, dear, you are the innocent one. We're going to make the most of this. If that Brown guy...well, he could...nothing...I guess." Her expression frowned, crumbled. "Oh, Eddy, it seems a damned dirty shame to destroy Benny just because of...well, if he hadn't escaped he wouldn't have done that and the girl would have been killed!"

"But the girl would never have crossed the street!" Edmund pointed out.

"That's not the point. The point is—well, that *ersatzes can* be more than chopping blocks for human emotions. That they *can* serve man in other ways and that they can-"

"*Stop!*" Edmund cried, laughingly. "You'll work yourself into a fit. And that's not what I came here to see. All 1 want is...the inside story on Benny."

"He was manufactured under normal circumstances—he came off the assembly line like thousands of *ersatzes*, nothing special about that, dear. Believe me! The only information you'll get from me will be slanted. In fact—from anybody here at the company. There are more secrets here than in D.C. You're searching up the wrong rocket tube."

Just then a buzzer rang at her desk. "Wait."

She went to the desk, pushed a button and a television screen slipped up into view. The face of a gray-haired man looked out from the three-dimension screen.

"Dr. Larson," Claire said. "What's the verdict?"

"We finished the lab tests—X-rayed the *ersatz*—negative. Nothing wrong," the man announced in a clipped voice. "From all indications, it's perfectly normal—except for the broken legs, but that could be repaired—under other circumstances. Are we to destroy it?"

"Not yet. I was told by the police to hold on to it...for a couple of hours at least."

The screen went dead and then folded back into the desk as Claire turned and faced Edmund.

"Do me a favor?" she pleaded, stepping close, sliding her arms around his neck, and pressing her body to his.

"When you ask like this...I don't know."

"Please...it means the world to me, please! Just this one little favor?" Her eyes pleaded, her lips pouted.

"What?" Edmund inquired, feeling the grinding sensation in his stomach again.

"When you go see Benny's owner, try to make him drop charges. Please...try to save Benny's *life.*"

She gently pressed against him in such a way that it was impossible for him to think straight. "I lied about the police. I wanted to buy time for Benny. You know the law...an *ersatz* who runs away is disposed of—automatically. Only if the owner steps in and-"

"Who the hell would try to save an *ersatz*? Hell, Claire, the whole purpose of your company is to sell as many as possible. Benny is disposed of—and they sell another to this guy. Who are you working for?"

"For the *ersatz*! And the company. If the law would change and we could...well selling *ersatzes* is only part of our business. Research & Development seeks a broader use for our product. Between the two of us we don't really need another sale—one way or the other. But just think about how it would change things if-"

"Oh, just thank God you aren't working for me—or, rather, I'm not your boss. I'd fire you!" he exclaimed, stepping away moving toward the door.

"No you wouldn't. It's all too complicated for your little reporter mind to understand, honey."

"The hell it is."

"Okay—we at the company would like to see things changed. The status of *Ersatz Inc.* is pretty complicated—but it is—for some of the members—pretty lousy. There's a power play going on. Up until now it has been pretty well balanced, but the liberals want to expand the area...build up a new branch...and that can only be done if a more liberal view is taken toward *ersatzes*. It'll be a long, hard battle—but if we can get our foot in the door—in time the *ersatzes* will have another place in the world and they'll be able to do more than be mere whipping dogs for human violence! If you could only get this guy to drop the charges...then we'd have something to work on—something which will set a new standard—from there on we can start a campaign to better the *ersatzes'* place in the world. Please, at least give it a try!"

"I'm not God! Claire, I don't have any power...I'm just a dumb reporter!"

"Hardly that. Even so...you'll be there on the ground floor with one-to-one connection when you interview him and...well..."

"I'll do what I can." He felt like a fool being twisted around her finger so easily, but realized there was little he wouldn't do for Claire. That's how much he loved her.

"Promise?"

"Promise!"

"Okay, get out of here, Eddy...I have work to do. I'm the one who has the headache of taking care of public relations."

"You're doing one hell of a job! No calls—a real busy woman!" he shot at her as he stepped to the door, which slid back automatically.

"Hell, the Cell has been blasting its head off all the time you've been here. I had the calls blocked so we wouldn't be interrupted," she laughed, returning to her desk. "See you later, love."

As Edmund walked down the white sparkling hallway, he felt a sense of depression and confusion.

Then another emotion ebbed upwards.

Maybe he could be sitting on a real-fire story. What if the owner released Benny? What if somebody took the case to court? What if the case was won, and Benny was allowed to live? What if a real big deal were made out of this? It would be the hottest story of the century! The law read very clear about the issue involved. It was a simple case of a machine going wrong—even if, in this case, there was a side effect. The fact remained that Benny had run away from his master. A defective piece of machinery. But if Benny were to take on a personality. Become a media personality. At this level the press had always had great power with the public. And Edmund didn't delude himself concerning his own influence—if an when he wanted to use it effectively.

What a story! And how easy to offer up that kind of material to his audience!

Edmund felt a wave of anger rush over him.

Damned Claire, she had caused him to think like her.

So it would be a story! But it was impossible. After all, this was simple enough—merely a human relations story.

Nothing more. Yet something warned him he was on the very edge of a deep leap across some kind of historical—if not hysterical—divide beyond which things would be forever changed.

One wrong move and …

He didn't want to think about that.

First he had to see the little girl Benny had saved.

CHAPTER THREE

Jeannie's father was a tall man with a kindly crinkling around his eyes. When he hurriedly stepped into the small home his family shared, his daughter rushed into his arms, tears bursting in her eyes.

"I want him—I want *him!*" she sobbed.

"Who is it you want?" he asked, puzzled, hugging her to him.

When the girl explained, her father turned surprised eyes at his attractive wife. "Did the policeman tell where they would take this *ersatz*?"

"No. He just told me what happened and I called you."

Ken Brown frowned and then considered. He was generally familiar with the law concerning *ersatzes*. He wondered if it would be possible to buy the one who had saved Jeannie's life. As he stood there, considering, the front doorbell rang. Ken opened the door, looked at the handsome dark haired man who was standing there.

"My name is Edmund Canfield, from the *National Star.* I was wondering if I could talk to your daughter about what happened this morning. I understand she was—"

"Come on in," Mr. Brown invited, stepping

back. The door closed behind the reporter.

Brown studied the man, taking in his broad shoulders, his level gaze and the sharp lines of his features, and decided he liked him. Ken Brown had always been one for snap decisions: and was seldom wrong. Here was a man who was sensitive, but firm when necessary

"You're *the* Edmund Canfield?" Mrs. Brown inquired in a high pitched, excited voice.

When Edmund nodded, she said: "I've followed your news stories for years...well, ever since you've been with the *National Star*. I've really enjoyed them!"

"Thanks, I'm glad that somebody does. My girl friend doesn't appreciate my editorials on the *ersatzes*...but she's a kook, a lovely one, but none the less!"

There was a short silence and then Mr. Brown said; "Maybe you could give me some information. You seem to know a lot about the *ersatz* situation, from what I've seen in your reports. This is my daughter's birthday...and, well, she wanted me to buy this *ersatz* who saved her life—you have any way of knowing how I might go about it?'

Edmund was thoughtful for a moment and then his eyes widened just slightly. He stood there before them like a man about to spring upon a prey. He felt as if he were about to leap over that valley to the other side of the endless plain of ultimate historical change! If he took this story to its final ending, designing its direction, it could literally change the political and social scene in totally unexpected ways. For some perverse reason he didn't care about anything but taking on this new challenge!

"Are you really serious about this?" Edmund inquired in a careful voice.

"Well...after all, it did save Jeannie's life. I can't think of a better one to get her." He hesitated and then added: "Maybe *I'm* a kook as you say—but I've always felt a...well, sorta strange about the *ersatzes*. It's almost as if they can really think. Well, that's beside the point. I've always tried to teach Jeannie to...well, be a nice little girl. We've always been a rather peaceful family. Not that we haven't had our violent moments...like everybody—I've lost my temper and taken it out on my *ersatz*—but I felt...well...ashamed afterwards. Silly, I know—"

Edmund laughed. nervously. "Don't worry, there are a lot of people like you. I managed to keep from having one, myself. No necessity. I roam around a lot, and...well—I don't go for this National Organization FREE—trying to humanize the *ersatz*—but..." He smiled.

Silence. Then, after a few awkward moments Mr. Brown said: "I'm serious about getting this *ersatz* for Jeannie. The more I think about this, the better it feels! Shouldn't be too difficult, should it?"

"I don't know. I haven't seen the owner, yet there are a lot of complications and—"

"I'll pay a good price...for that matter."

"There's the law, you know. This...Benny... that's what he's being called now—well, he ran away, as you know. The law reads pretty clear on that. A defective machinery. The *ersatz* is made for a certain purpose and well, this Benny revolted." He shrugged, feeling uncertain: "I know, that's sounding crazy. How can a machine revolt! Well, never mind that. They'll dispose of it, unless the owner will step in."

"Daddy, Daddy!" Jeannie cried, rushing up to her father. "Please, I want him...I want him! I want him!" Tears ran down her little flushed cheeks and her body shook, against his as if the world had suddenly come to an end.

The father shrugged, looked at Edmund Canfield. "Is there anything we can do?"

"You could try contacting the owner, I'm going over to see him in any case. You could come with me." Edmund had already forgotten about the interview he'd come to get.

"Okay." Brown turned to his little girl and smiled, patting her head. "Don't worry...I'll see what can be done about this."

* * * * * * *

The small, one-unit house was in the cheap rent slum district. There was a foul smell in the air of soot and sulfur. The houses. packed tightly together. consisted of metal walls around three small rooms. As Edmund stepped up to the door with Jeannie Brown's father at his side. he felt an edge' of excitement rushed through him.

Already he was more involved in this situation than he'd planned. But the impulsive, almost instinctive reaction to the sudden turn of events had sparked the reporter instinct in him. A story—a really BIG one—was on the edge of breaking. If Ken Brown decided to take his daughter's plea seriously enough, it would make headlines for weeks. He'd be in on the ground floor.

A voice asked from the door-speaker. "Who is

it?"

"Edmund Canfield of the *National Star*. We want to talk to Mr. Adams."

There was a moment of silence and then the door slowly slid open. They walked into a dimly lighted room. There wasn't any of the auto overhead lighting so common throughout most sections of the city. Poorness played through every inch of the place, from its cheap wallpaper to the worn, tattered furniture that must have been half a dozen years old.

The woman who was sitting on the soft, padded chair in the corner, looked worn, tired, old. Her hair was gray streaked, and loose around her shoulders. The lines in her face were traced thinly around her mouth, eyes, across her wide forehead. She couldn't be more than thirty-five, but there was an oldness about her that must have been there for years.

"Yes? What can I do for you?" she inquired. not standing, just sitting there looking at them.

"I want to see Mr. Adams," Edmund announced.

"He's not here right now. Can I do anything for you?"

It was Mr. Brown who spoke.

"I want to buy your *ersatz*. I can pay a good price for him."

The woman stared at him for a long time before saying anything. Finally she stood. Her face hardened. "That Benny he'll be the death of me, yet"

Silence, then she continued. "I couldn't tell you anything—I don't have the authority. I'm sorry. My husband is being questioned by the authorities."

Edmund looked at his watch and then at Brown. "We don't have much time. They go through an automatic operation. There's been a delay for a short time Miss Richards is doing what she can to save the *ersatz*."

Mrs. Adams blinked at them. "I don't understand. Why would anybody want to save Benny?"

"Because he saved my daughter's life!" Brown announced finally.

Mrs. Adams shrugged. "As far as I'm concerned they can get rid of him! I don't see that it matters much—but I'll talk to my husband about it."

Edmund looked at his watch again. "Look Brown, if we were to go to the High Court of Records...we could get a restraining order until papers can be signed. I should have thought of that before. We don't have much time."

They said good-bye to Mrs. Adams and returned to Edmund's ground-car.

As they were speeding away toward the center of the city, Ken Brown turned and asked Edmund: "Do you really think...well, I'm being silly about this? After all, what's the difference? One *ersatz* is as good as another!"

"Don't ask me. I'll advise you on all questions except that one! I'm...pulling for Benny...but only as a reporter. It could be a hot story. Personally I can't help thinking too much is being made of the whole damn thing."

Edmund watched the traffic shooting along the automatically controlled roadway. He lighted a cigarette, put his feet high on the control board, pressed a button which dropped the seat back. He lounged there, thinking about what was happening, finding it hard to believe that it *was* actually happening.

Ersatzes were nothing but highly developed robots, machines, like ground-cars—nothing more.

Yet there was the other side—the side which Claire Richards preached. Were they truly something more? There were some people who believed so— Mr. Brown was on the edge of belief and acting as if he believed. Perhaps that was merely an act, or a self-delusion developing in defense of taking this action in the name of his daughter.

"There might be a fight in this!" Edmund pointed out.

"What kind of fight? After all—an *ersatz* is an *ersatz*—just as a washing machine is a washing machine. What's the difference? Why should there be any difference?" But it was a question more stated in wonderment, than mere conviction; more as if the man wanted some answer which made sense.

"I don't know. But something warns me that this is going to be bigger than either of us realize," Edmund announced.

The car turned, slid to the night side of the road, up a circular ramp around and up to the side of the High Courts Building. A moment later it came to a stop in the parking lot, automatically cutting itself off. The doors opened.

"Well here goes nothing!" Edmund sighed.

As Brown got out of the car, he looked at Edmund for a fall minute, his eyes distant, slowly hardening.

"You know, Canfield, I think maybe I might really get serious about this if it got to a fight! I don't know, exactly, why. But…once I make up my mind about something…well, I can get pig-headed!"

"How serious are you?" Edmund inquired, firing the question like a bullet. "We best know, right now!"

"I don't know. But suddenly...well, this whole *ersatz* thing is so new. Just a few years, really, if you consider. Okay, decade. But historically...just a half-heart beat. And, well, I wonder if maybe some things have been overlooked. Those nuts, crying 'equal rights' for *ersatzes*—that's just what those fanatical FREE folk are—nuts. But...does that mean *ersatzes* have to be mere whipping dogs—or that they have to be considered mere machines? I don't know. This is just as if it were meant to happen— that's the way I feel about it. Like we were being moved in some gigantic chess game, like some Gods were playing out a drama and we're in the middle of it—the feature actors."

They stood there for a moment and then started for the large entrance to the Court of Records.

* * * * * * *

Judge Thomas, Judge of the High Court of Records, was a heavy man in his middle fifties. He had sat on the bench for a little over twenty years, a fact which several people in high office were making a big point of. There was rumor that in the coming election—only a few weeks ahead—he might be unseated by a younger man named Carlton Chambers. It wasn't necessarily a serious threat, but one which he had to contend with in a serious manner. Anything he did in the next weeks could be of great importance. Any mistake would be used against him; a big enough mistake would give him a quick, instant retirement plan.

He was just getting ready to close court when the Court Officer came up and told him there was a Mr. Edmund Canfield and Mr. Ken Brown there to

48

see him.

"Bring them in," he instructed.

The court room was small, no more than twenty by twenty feet; but large enough for the legal matters which the State had put in his charge. The walls were illustrated in lovely flat-painted scenes of ancient missions which had at one time lined the California coast. Somebody, many years before, had taken a liking to those images, and whoever had painted them on the walls and done so in a tastefully muted manner. It all gave the illusion of warmth and comfort; something of a lie considering the hard issues hammered out before the Law. Decisions made in this room could shatter a human like as if it were a mere bug to be brutally squashed.

Judge Thomas was aware of the power his position had over those who came before him.

Two men stepped into the room. One was dark haired, the other Thomas had seen several times before in the papers: Ken Brown, a very well established businessman.

"Present your case," the Court Officer said to the two men.. "The Honorable Judge Tom B. Thomas is presiding." The man flicked a switch on the side wall and the Court Reporter, a built-in mechanical M-brain, hummed alive. "Case 2-B—77946, of June 12, 2075."

Judge Thomas looked grimly down at the two men, his mind only half alive to what they were about to say. He was thinking about his wife, about his children, who were planning a vacation trip to South America for the weekend—a trip which he was looking forward to with excitement.

The sandy haired man stepped forward and addressed Judge Thomas.

"I wish to request a restraining order on the disposal of an *ersatz*."

The judge's mind snapped to attention. He stared at the man, feeling a sudden alarm. "Would you mind explaining?"

"Well, your honor," Brown said, "I...it was in the papers today. The *ersatz* who ran away saved my daughter's life and it's her birthday and I wanted to buy the *ersatz* for her." The man looked down at his feet, his face flushed. "I know this all sounds rather...odd."

"At least!" The judge huffed up, a bit annoyed. "And somewhat insane. No! Mad!"

Edmund Canfield stepped quickly forward. "Your honor, could I speak up here?"

"I wish you would!" The judge felt an icy hand tickle his spine.

"I'm actually only an interested bystander but I'm covering this story for the National Star telepaper and know the particulars involved. A Miss Claire Richards, of *Ersatz* Inc., has held off the disposal of the *ersatz* in the hopes that the owner will place a restraining order and claim that Benny..."

"Now who's that?"

"That's the name of this particular *ersatz*!"

"Name? Of...the *ersatz*?"

"Well, many people do give names to their pet-"

"I know all about that. I'm not without my own ... well, experience with those...well..."

"Well, then, sir, this Miss Richards, of *Ersatz* Inc., can hold off the auto destruction just so long without your help. If we can get him to state that Benny didn't run away...it might hold things off..."

"You mean...pervert the law?"

"No. Sir. Just prevent a miscarriage of justice."

"I'd debate that with you if I had the time. I don't. Just want is it you want."

"Well, if you could help us...with the restraining order holding off automatic destruction..."

"And?"

"Mr. Brown wants to buy him from the owner."

The judge was silent for a moment, considering. This was a matter he would rather not be troubled with. Re-election was too close. One move in the wrong direction could ruin his career. Normally such a situation wouldn't arouse any public opinion. But Ken Brown was high enough in the business world to make a big stink, and the media would play the event up as a big human interest story involving the well-to-do businessman. The fact that Edmund Canfield was involved was enough to prove that last fact.

"Who owns the *ersatz*?'

"A Mr. Adams," Brown announced.

"And you wish to purchase it from this man?" the judge asked, making sure that his words were pronounced clearly, so the Recorder would tape it down without flaw.

"Yes. My daughter wants him." Brown showed irritation on his face. His features grew tight and red. "How much red tape do I have to go through? This is a *special* case. I know about the law involved...but, after all, aren't laws made to bend? Certainly this isn't of any great issue! I merely want to buy an *ersatz* for my daughter. Does it matter from whom I get it?"

"Don't you think this is hardly a very important

matter? One *ersatz* is as good as another. What difference does it make?" the judge asked.

"Let's say it's a matter of principle. This one saved Jeannie's life. For that reason alone I believe it has a right to...'live'."

Judge Thomas felt rage burst up through him. "God, man—these creatures don't have life—they're synmen. They have no feelings—no awareness other than what we give them."

The expression on the other man's face convinced the judge that he was quite serious.

"It's enough that my daughter wants him. What harm is there in it? Just one *ersatz*. I'll pay the owner a good price. I need a restraining order to stop the automatic destruction. Otherwise, even if that man signs the release papers it'll be too late!" Brown's eyes hardened.

"Believe me, you're wasting your time. I can give you the order—but it'll merely hold off the inevitable. The Law reads *very clear* on this point. Very clear indeed."

"I don't care what the damned law reads about this. It's my right as a *Citizen* to *demand* the restraining order. If I thought it was necessary to have a lawyer I'd have called J. B. Harrington."

Judge Thomas reacted to that statement. Harrington's reputation as a lawyer was nationwide; his political pull fantastic. It was also public knowledge that Brown was very close to the man. If Harrington came into the picture there was little doubt that a national incident would be made of the whole affair. An incident he didn't want at the present time.

He tried once more: "You're wasting your time and mine, believe me."

Brown's face tightened harder. The lines set, determined. "Can I use your televisor? I'll call Harrington, and we'll see whose time is being wasted. I made a legal demand—and I expect it followed!"

The judge sighed and nodded, his temper and frustration getting the best of him, letting fury show in his choice of words, instantly recorded: "Okay, okay! I'll call the damn Syn-Lab, requesting the holding order on the bloody *ersatz*."

CHAPTER FOUR

When they returned to the ground-car, Edmund looked at the man beside him, amazed.

"You really put on the heat!"

Brown laughed nervously. "It surprised me a little, too. I don't know what got into me! Back to Adam's place?"

Edmund entered Adam's address and then pressed the activator button and the car slipped automatically out of the parking space and headed down the ramp, then once on the ground level turned in the direction of Adam's home.

"Are you really serious now?" Edmund inquired.

"Quite!" Brown announced stubbornly.

"All the way?"

"I believe so."

"For the paper...this is going to be a big story!" Edmund told him.

The news story flashed onto all the telescreens, in the normal text or voice, across the world:

ERSATZ BENNY DESIRED
BY GIRL'S FATHER

Judge Tom Thomas signed a restraining order for the *ersatz* named Benny, who saved the life of Jeannie Brown this morning. Her father, Ken Brown, the well-to-do business executive, working for *International Insurance, Inc.*, requested the restraining order for the *ersatz*, with the purpose of buying it from its owner, Mr. Smithington Adams, from whom it had apparently run away the night before.

Judge Thomas, upon being questioned, said, "I don't see the reasoning behind this man's thinking. The law is very clear on this point. *Ersatzes*, like any other piece of machinery, are disposed of automatically when proven defective. I attempted to talk Mr. Brown out of this action. I wash my hands of the affair. I'm sure that this man will realize the mistake he's making and withdraw his order."

The man in question, Mr. Ken Brown, stated that he is determined to purchase this *ersatz* as a birthday present for his daughter, who turned seven today. He was quoted as saying that it only seemed fair that Benny be saved, considering that the *ersatz* saved his daughter's life.

Ersatz Inc. is officially quiet on the matter and refuses to make any statements to the press. Though an insider indicated that they are quite pleased and hope that the Browns will fight this through to the end.

Upon talking to Mr. Adams, the man claimed he would have nothing to do with the situation. There is rumor that some unknown people in high office had influenced him. He simply stated that as far as he was concerned, the *ersatz* was—to quote—"defective and should be done away with." Beyond that, he refused to make any statements.

It is not known, as yet, what will become of Benny—or how far it might be necessary to go through legal courts to settle the case.

Mr. Brown, from all indications, seems quite willing to fight all the way in order to have Benny saved from automatic disposal.

It would seem that in order to take possession of Benny from the State, it would be necessary to fight in the High Court—and possibly fight—the law as it now stands.

The question which is at issue here is if an *ersatz*, who can take the unusual action of saving a girl's life, is defective in the normal sense of the word. Since the main function of *ersatzes* is to serve as emotional whipping blocks for violence, to provide a release against violence, which the law punishes when inflicted on a human being, and not for the purpose of saving lives, or serving man in any other function, it would seem that the *ersatz* named Benny is malfunctioning, and therefore defective.

The National Organization FREE made a statement through its normal channels to the effect that this case proved beyond a doubt that *ersatzes* could and would serve man in a far more reaching way than originally designed if the law and the public attitude were changed.

Mayor Sherman of Los Angeles was approached on the subject but refused any more statement than to say, "Brown's an idiot!"

At this moment nobody knows for sure what will happen. FREE hasn't, as yet, contacted Mr. Brown, and it would seem that they aren't about to do more than make their normal verbal statements. Like most organizations, they are more noise than action. It might be interesting to know what they would do if this comes to a real legal fight.

Edmund watched the story as his car drove through town toward Mark Palmer's large Bel Air home. He shuddered as he read some of the last statements about FREE and wondered if he had, in the flare of creative heat, been a little too forceful about them. If Claire ever found out that it was his story, sparks would fly. He hated to think about it.

The city was spread across the land much like

most modern cities of the twenty-first century. Miles and miles of land were crowded with tall sky-scrapers which reached into the clouds. Some were two and three hundred stories high. The roadways lined through the skyways, every twenty levels, cutting into and through the tall buildings. Only in the living quarters of the very poor and the very rich were buildings only one or two stories high; but even these were quickly being torn down and re-placed with skyscrapers in the frantic attempt to keep up with the ever zooming population. In another twenty years it was expected that only the very, very rich would own land.

Los Angeles had spread in the last hundred years to cover all the territory up to within a few miles of San Francisco, which took the Northern California under its government wing. In the west, Los Angeles stopped reluctantly at the ocean but spread out down to include San Diego; to the east it sprawled to the edge of Arizona and Nevada. Almost an endless sea of buildings were piled one after another, sprinkled by the low poor sections and the homes of the very rich. The city had grown out around these older sections, ignoring them because of the expanse of land that had stretched unused for so many years before. Now there was little place to build other than up; and the eating away of the older sections; time would do this. Population Control had slowed the expansion problem for only a short time. Smog-control—through the use of electrically run engines—had made the cities, with its multitude of clogged road and air-ways, livable. Auto controlled traffic made it possible to move from one destination to another by direct dialing—otherwise nobody would be able to find their way through the maze of endless buildings without getting lost forever.

Edmund's eyes were attracted to the telescreen news as another *ersatz* story silently flashed on the screen:

NOTED DOCTOR SPEAKS ON THE *ERSATZ* SITUATION—REV. G. CLAY BELMONT

In regard to this foolish action, which Mr. Brown has taken tonight, it seems only proper that I make a public statement about what he is actually suggesting.

If—and that is a big if—he were to take this issue seriously, and fight the standing law, it is quite possible that our already overcrowded living conditions will be even more of a problem than they now are.

Consider, if you will, how over the last few decades the public has been forced to accept legalized birth control as a *way-of-life* rather than an intelligent choice of each and every couple. Such restrictive laws have been forced upon humanity—against the will of any morally aware person—because we *had* to bring an end to the population expansion that was eating away our food-growing lands. It was a choice between creeping starvation or survival for those who already live. There wasn't any choice. Even the Church of

Rome was forced to sign a statement urging this law be passed, rather than see billions of human beings starving. Today a couple can't have children without expressed permission from the government; only two per couple at *most!*

As one Senator, to remain unknown, said:

"It is simply a crime—and morally degenerate sin, in my mind—to have more than one child per person. Criminal, disgusting, and down right selfish! This law, and stronger, should have been brought about in the twentieth century! It is about time that these perverts, these human rabbits reproducing more of their disgusting baby rabbits, be stopped at the groins! I'd castrate them! I literally believe we should have a woman's tubes tied when she gives birth to her first child! That would fix things. Shut down the baby-making factory. Hell, if you must, fix the husband, too! Clip it all in the bud! In fact, I'm pushing for such a simply, uncomplicated law! And the blue noses, those criminals who talk about religious rights to multiply 'cause that's what it says in the Bible, continue to attempt to lobby for unrestricted births! They disgust me to the core! Well, they'll have to get past me! And I'm pushing hard to tighten up the present laws! We must put an end to the Rabble Rabbits!"

Such equally blunt statements are offered by the Religious Right, and they don't include merely the western Christian religions. But the battle continues.

Even then, with illegal births, the rate of population explosion has not been stopped. There are rumors that in only a few years the governments of the world will once again enact a World Law, restricting birth to no more than one child for every married couple, much as our "unnamed" famous Senator has so brazenly stated.

At the rate we are now going, the human race shall be cut in half *by law!* It is necessary for survival. That's the logic behind such strong anti-birth laws.

The dream of mankind reaching for the stars as a solution to over-population has died with the realization that it is actually *impossible* to ship that many human beings from our planet to another—even if there were such worlds to be settled.

The twenty-first century has brought these deadly cold facts to light.

We are, for the time being, at least, restricted to this planet Earth and the small colonies on the Moon, Mars and the outer moons of the Big Planets. Exploration of Deep Space is still more a dream than reality insofar as a solution of human survival. Time will give Deep Space to man—if we *survive that long!*

So we have had to face certain realities, one of which is control of our population to hold down human expansion until logical solutions can be developed.

And now we have this man attempting to give legal status to *ersatzes*! In a world already ripped apart by over-crowding.

That is madness!

Sure, some say that *ersatzes* don't eat food. They don't! It is claimed they could be used to do other activities—to serve man as working slaves. But we have computers, robotic devices that do much of the mass work of keeping civilization running smoothly. And there aren't enough meaningful jobs for the majority of human beings. Creative arts just don't offer the answer as a good outlet to man's inner and outer needs.

So, can you imagine, if you will, *ersatzes* being given full rights, like human beings? Now, of course, this is quite impossible, but consider the situation in light of our crowded living conditions. Please do! Where would the *ersatzes* go? What would happen to our cities?

But of course this will not happen,

for no man, not even this Mr. Brown, would think of giving full rights to the *ersatzes*. After all, they are only machines. Yet exactly what is at issue here?

Do we reward the washing machine for doing its job? Do we reward it for breaking down and revolting? No!

Edmund clicked off the mediavision and then settled back, puffed a cigarette until it glowed and then took a deep drag.

He was sitting on a moment of history which could splash into all sorts of complications, a story that was about to upset the whole balance of society. He felt the implications of what was happening—for which he was partly responsible.

Angrily he reached to the control panel, punched out a Rocket Rum, and when the cocktail slipped out of the little opening in the panel, he gulped it down. He ordered another and was just finishing it off when the car turned down a privately marked side road and came to a stop outside a large, sprawling home which reached three stories high.

The door opened and he got out.

A few moments later he stepped into the house behind the butler who had answered the door for him.

The loud sound of music filled the house, coming from the second floor, which he knew to be a large ballroom. Mixed with the blare of modern symphony jazz was the loud murmuring of voices chattering endlessly at one another. But there was a buzz which he could hear even from the hallway; a buzz which repeated the words *ersatz* and Benny, as if the combined mass of conversation were blending together to form one voice.

He turned to the butler, who was a well built young man in his middle twenties.

"Did a Miss Richards leave a message for me?"

"I'll see." The man disappeared into a little office and then returned a few moments later. "Yes...if you're Edmund Canfield."

Edmund nodded.

"She said to meet her at the bar."

* * * * * * *

Edmund walked down the hall to the L-tube and a moment later stepped into a huge, crowded room. The noise was like Las Vegas at New Year's Eve. He forced his way through the packed people toward the large wall to wall bar on the far side of the room. A live band was playing to the left, on a stage set up for this purpose.

The moment he reached the bar, Edmund found a control panel and pushed a button that ordered a *Galactic High Ball,* which he downed quickly. Then he punched for another, turning and looking along the paneled counter which was decorated much like the bars that had been in fashion during the mid-nineteenth century. It was a festive arrangement, with a short space between the bar counter and the wall. On the wall had been painted a likeness of rows on rows of liquor bottles, most of which had been out of circulation for decades, ever since the invention of the automatic bar mixers that were in fashion nowadays. Every three feet, on the counter, were arranged the control panel to serve out drinks at the touch of a fingertip. Still, the general atmosphere was enjoyably old fashioned and actually quite comfortable—a very popular *décor* for public saloons.

The people crowded around the room were dressed in high fashion The men were in the tailored suits that had cycled back to the open vest and jacket, almost like those in the middle, a perfect match to the bar setting. The women had on low cut gowns that exposed as much breast-flesh as polite society allowed. The colors were vivid and flashy, from bright greens to flushed red to cool blues.

He took the second drink and headed toward the bandstand where he was sure Claire would have placed herself. She loved music with the same passion that she did sex and the *ersatzes*—though not necessarily in that order.

It took him only a moment to spot her, standing by the bar, her eyes fastened to the twenty piece band blaring away on its Latin jazz rhythm.

Claire was dressed in pink silk; draped over her body in a much more respectable way than he was used to seeing her. The neckline dipped low enough to be intriguing, but not overly seductive. Her hair was loose over bare shoulders.

Edmund stepped close and caressed her neck with a light kiss.

Claire jumped as if shot.

"God!" she cried, turning. "I thought you weren't going to get here at all!"

"It's hardly nine-twenty. Miss the ballet?"

"No as usual they are late in starting. I heard that the Palmers had a fight over the *ersatz* issue and aren't talking." She snickered and her eyes sparkled as they looked up into his.

"You've been drinking!" he accused in a mockingly scolding voice.

"Of course. Martinis!"

"Martini? What's that?"

"Mark Palmer told me about them. They were popular during the nineteen hundreds. A cocktail combination of gin and vermouth. Why don't you try one? They're a little...well, bitter, I guess you might say. Anyway, Mark said they are one of the strongest drinks made—something about the combination being chemically powerful—I don't know."

She giggled and then punched at the control panel at her side. "He programmed the bar for them—trying to start a new fad, he said. Maybe it will take!" She handed him a small cup which held about three ounces of liquor.

"Are you kidding?" Edmund cried. "Couldn't you have made it a little bigger?"

"That's the way they come, Eddy. Believe me—you'll be surprised—hey! Don't gulp them..."

Edmund emptied the cup in two swallows and the liquor burned down his throat. For a moment he stood there, on the verge of choking. The taste that filled his mouth was salty and oily. He waited for the effect and when it didn't come, he nodded to Claire.

"One more of your bite size drinks."

A moment later she gave him another, grinning mischievously.

"You'll be sorry!" she teased in a high pitched warning voice.

"That little thing?"

He gulped. This time he felt it go down all the way like an icy fire. For a moment he stood there, waiting, afraid, knowing that a bomb was about to explode in his brain.

Then it happened. Something knocked the back of his head like a hammer, then blasted upwards, and a moment later slowly ebbed its way along his skull, downwards through every nerve in his body.

"Say—that's all right!" He pulled Claire close, kissed her lips.

"Not in public!" she scolded, embarrassed, pushing him playfully away.

"Did you see the news?" Edmund inquired, hoping she hadn't guessed that he'd written the report.

Claire managed the impossible by both frowning and smiling at the same time.

"Is this Mr. Brown really serious?" she asked.

"As far as I know."

Her eyes lighted. "I *knew*—just knew there was a reason to celebrate! Everybody here at the party has been talking about it. It looks like two radically different attitudes have locked horns. Either they think Brown is an idiot or they're praising him to the planets. It's exciting!"

Suddenly the music came to an end and a large man with a red, bloated face stepped up on the small make-shift stage.

"Quiet everybody."

"Look at him," Claire said, nudging Edmund in the ribs. "Mark Palmer is mad—look at his eyes...ever see him like that before?"

"What's wrong?"

"I told you—an argument with his wife. He came home in a rage about the...news story. He thought Brown was raving mad. When his wife announced she thought it was wonderful what the man was doing for his little girl—bubbling over the whole story about Benny—Mark hit the ceiling, called one of his *ersatzes*, pulled out a knife and slit its belly open. Rose was furious and told him so. I understand they really had a fight. Mark took it out on a couple more *ersatzes* and happened to pick on one of the dancers and so they had to program another." Claire had spoken in soft whispers, and by the time she was finished a muddy silence had fallen on the room.

Mark Palmer stood there looking at the thin mike floating in front of him. For a moment he didn't say anything. Then, taking a deep breath, said:

"A lot of you people are personal friends—some I hardly know—but you were all invited here to see an *ersatz ballet* and party it up." He coughed nervously, looked in the direction of a lovely redhead who was standing a few feet away—Rose Palmer. Fire sparked the air between the two.

"Originally," he continued in a tight voice, "things were supposed to get started a little earlier, but...as a matter of fact—" He broke off long enough to throw a glance back at his wife.

"As a matter of fact I imagine several of us here have had some strong reactions—on a personal level—over this *ersatz* story."

There was a tittering from the crowded room. Several laughed out loud, some shouted angrily or in good humor.

"I'm not going to make any editorial type statements—" Palmer quickly inserted. "Only that something happened to one of the ballet dancers and…well, we had to program another."

Another tittering flashed across the room.

Somebody close by said in a small voice, just loud enough so that Edmund and Claire could hear: "I bet he cut the thing's neck open!"

Claire turned and glared at the man who had spoken. "You'd think people would learn!" she said to Edmund.

"Learn what?"

"That *ersatzes* are—"

"Not now!"

Palmer was speaking and Edmund turned his attention to the man.

"The ballet is a contemporary number, concerning two women and a man. The woman in white represents Julie, true romantic love—the love of life and love itself. She is in love with the man, and he with her. But the woman in the mask, Carol, comes between them. She is determined to have the man—and will do anything to gain him. Even to the point of making love to the woman in white. And in the end our pure blonde haired beauty wins out—to prove love is all…and wins all. The lights will be lowered, and I must request that everybody move back along the walls…there will be room for everybody, if you'll just squeeze back a little. The floor will lower to make terraced steps so that you'll all be able to get a good view. I hope you enjoy the production."

As he stepped down from the stage, the center floor cleared away as people backed toward the walls. Once the floor was empty, it slowly lowered and, dropping in sections, created a six step terraced stairway along the four walls.

People adjusted themselves as the lights slowly dimmed to semi-darkness.

The musicians on the bandstand opened with a jazzy fanfare and the bass picked up the beat, followed by bongo drums.

The lights brightened slightly to a dim red glow which filled the room. A hazy force field settled down from the ceiling like the lowering of a shimmering curtain, in front of the audience lining the four walls. It was possible to see in to the center floor "stage," but beyond that the audience beyond became mere shadow figures against red.

The red glow grew brighter, then a spotlight shined to the left of the room, revealing a concert grand piano, behind which sat an *ersatz* who played a series of musical runs on the keyboard.

A blonde female *ersatz* wearing a white, long evening dress, ran across the room from the right, coming to the piano, sliding her arms around the man's neck, embracing him, kissing his cheek and then his mouth as he turned.

They stood, danced across the floor in time with the music which had taken a waltz tempo. They danced for several minutes, and then as the band suddenly blared into a driving vamp, a "woman" in black tights which hugged her voluptuous figure like an outer layer of skin, wearing long black gloves, with a black mask over her face, entered from behind the piano.

The dancers stopped, froze, and then slowly turned.

The blonde woman backed away from her partner, terror lighting her beautiful features.

The woman in black charged forward, spinning, reaching out for the woman in white.

"Julie...you are mine!" a voice spoke from the mask.

"No! No! Never!" Julie screamed, running from one side of the room to the other, always followed by the woman in tights. "Leave me leave me alone!"

Julie disappeared from the room.

The man turned, watching the masked woman.

"Why'd you do that, Carol?"

"Why not! I want you!"

Carol danced around the man, reached for him, pressed herself close, and he relaxed in her arms. They kissed and then danced around the room until they exited to the right.

Julie re-entered, searched through imaginary rooms, twirling, dancing, and leaping in the air.

Edmund lost interest, turned, kissed Claire the neck.

"Don't!" Claire demanded.

"You really like this show?"

"It's beautiful!"

"So much for..." He didn't finish the statement.

Disgusted, he whispered: "I'm getting out of here for a while."

"Meet me here?" she inquired.

"In a little while."

Edmund made his way through the massed people to a side door and found himself in a small room.

Mark Palmer was standing there, talking to a large balding man. Both men were red-faced from heavy boozing.

For a moment Edmund stood there trying to remember where he had seen the other man. Then he remembered. J. B. Harrington, the famous lawyer.

CHAPTER FIVE

Mark Palmer spotted Edmund first. "Well, I was wondering if you were here."

Edmund smiled, "I hear you had a little difficulty this evening."

"That out, already?"

"Well, Claire told me something—"

"Oh, I did mention it to her. How'd she like the Martinis? I couldn't be sure—one of those old fashioned drinks—she seemed to like them-"

"Recommended it to me. Quite a kick!"

Mark Palmer laughed and then said: "This is Harrington. Have you two met?"

J. B. Harrington turned, looked at Edmund, frowned, then grinned and extended his hand.

"I've read your news stories with interest, young man!" Harrington announced, gripping his hand.

"I follow your cases—"

"Well, that's over. The polite openings! What about this *ersatz* thing? Is Brown really..."

"Serious? Everybody asks me that! He mentioned your name today to Judge Thomas—the judge was reluctant to give the order..."

Harrington laughed, a bellowing laughter that came from deep within his barrel chest. "Election year. Nobody wants to mess with something that is in the least bit touchy. And that touched off a storm. Every mother in the nation is pulling for Benny."

A short silence, then Harrington stared into Edmund's eyes. "That story was yours?"

"What story?"

"The one on television this evening. Had your style." The eyes narrowed knowingly.

"Don't tell anybody, I have problems, too. Claire Richards works for *Ersatz Inc.*—has a soft spot for them...if she knew..." Edmund put a finger to his lips, indicating silence.

Mark Palmer grinned. "Not a word will utter from my lips, Ed."

Harrington was thoughtful for a moment, then his chest heaved. He said: "It is a rather ticklish subject. If Brown fights it—and he'll *have* to—it could be a bloody mess. Rocket sparks all over the place."

"Exactly what would it involve?" Edmund inquired carefully.

"For the media...it'll be an issue on a minor point of law. It's minor in the level that it's *almost* unwritten law. But it is in writing, and that makes it important. Public opinion will have a lot to do with it. Any lawyer trying to argue such a case would be faced with the problem of...well, like trying to make a change in the law about..." He stood there thoughtfully for a moment, then said: "The legal rights of ground-cars—or better yet, of computer brains!" A bright, amused grin spread across his features. "Actually...not for the media—it'll involve the issue of what is a man—what is a soul—what makes up a personality—a thinking, reasoning personality. *That's* why it's a messy situation."

"Brown's a friend of yours. Would you help him

if he approached you?" Edmund asked.

Harrington shook his head, not to the question itself, but more on the whole subject. "Brown is, between you and me, a nice guy. But I don't think he knows what he's getting into. I wouldn't know what my reactions would be. I haven't really given it much thought."

There was a long, drawn out silence which slowly became awkward. Harrington shrugged, pulled out a cigar, puffed it light and then said: "If you'll excuse me—I understand this ballet ends with a bang!"

Mark Palmer managed to look pleased. "The lady in black gets her just rewards." Then he added: "I changed the ending—Rose will blast a rocket tube!"

The three returned to the ballroom.

On "stage" were two women. Julie was now dressed in white bra and panties. The other woman was struggling with her, trying to pull her off the floor.

Mark Palmer nudged Edmund. "In a moment!"

The lights flared, like red lightning. Six *ersatz-men* charged across the floor, circled around the two women, and then Carol stepped away, out through the circle of men.

The men edged forward.

Then from beyond the piano the hero entered, a gun in his hand. He fired, fired again and again, each time hitting one of *ersatzes*, who jerked back as the bullets tore gaping, bloody looking holes in their bodies.

A combined shout of approval sounded from the audience.

The man turned to Carol, glided smoothly to-wards her, pulled out a knife, then threw it to Julie, who caught it in mid-air.

The two women circled each other. Carol was suddenly in possession of a long whip which lashed through the air, striking at Julie's bare back, cutting a red streak across it.

Edmund moved through the crowd toward Claire, as the audience shouted in excitement.

As he came to Claire he heard a low, agonized scream and turned to see Julie step back from the woman in black. A knife was sticking in Carol's belly, red "blood" already beginning to stream out.

Edmund looked away. He had seen such shows many times in the past and they usually left him unmoved. But now, for the first time, he felt an emotional reaction, completely different from the excited thrill which had surged through him as a younger man seeing his first *ersatz* ballet. Some of them were even more violent, and many quite erotic in their graphic sexual interplay.

What if ersatzes were "human"? What if they really felt? Pain. Terror. Even sexual feelings? What if they were super human in their hungers and needs?

He shoved the thoughts away and slid an arm around Claire's waist.

"Let's get out of here!" he suggested. "We might find some cozy little place all alone."

She turned, her eyes moist, tears running down them. "I didn't know...they would..."

Her voice choked.

She hugged him and then nodded. "Let's do get out of here!'

They pushed their way through the crowd and then left the room. A few moments later they were stepping outside into the night air.

"Oh...God!" Claire moaned. "I never want—to see anything like that again!"

"Claire...don't get all worked up...we want to have a beautiful evening." The flare of emotion which sparked in her eyes made him say. "I love you...and I don't want to think about...well, about the—"

She placed a delicate finger on his lips and smiled. "Okay—how about a spin? I feel like doing something that will take the taste out of my mind and mouth."

"What would you suggest?"

"The Stellar Hotel?" she suggested, pressing her fingers into his arm.

"From one sin spot to another?" he laughed.

"What's so sinful about gambling?"

"It costs money!"

She frowned. "I have my own—if that's bothering you."

"Claire—I'm not a poor man, you know."

Their ground-car came down the ramp and stopped in front of them, the door opening. They got in, and the doors closed.

"I haven't been there in ages. Their rooms are fantastic!" she cried excitedly, as he punched out their destination.

"Gambling, gaming, and party-time! Why not? You can really have a ball!" Edmund exclaimed, pulling her close.

He touched a button on the control panel and the windows clouded gray black, letting no light in or out. The seats slipped back, slid together with the backseats, stretched out until there was a low, comfortable padded bedding under them.

"Why, Eddy, for shame!" she teased; mocking him with a frown.

"Don't you think it's a wonderful idea?" he inquired. "Get us warmed up for the Stellar action!"

"Do I need warming up?

"Never, but it is fun trying to!" he chuckled.

The Martini cocktails had done their work on both of them, and now the sudden surge of passion sparked into a roaring flame, licking frantically at their nerves.

As the ground-car sped through the city towards the Stellar Hotel, some fifty miles from the Palmer home, the two played out their lover's game.

Finally they moved away from each other. For a long time they lay there, trapped in their own thoughts.

Edmund knew what he wanted; knew what he needed more than anything else in the world—to love Claire as a wife, as the only woman in his life, from that moment on. He was just going to suggest they get married, when Claire sat up and said, "Isn't there something we can do about this *ersatz* thing?"

"*What!*" he exclaimed, almost angrily, startled, trying to hide the disappointment from his voice.

"Don't have to shout!" she scolded almost teasingly.

He forced a shrug, offered: "Well…what?"

"You could start writing things...well, pointing out *his* side. Build the story up so that the public will see it Benny's way." She pleaded with her eyes.

"I don't know..." Edmund was thoughtful for a

moment.

"Didn't that mean anything to you—what that *ersatz* ballet turned into? What if they did feel—the same way we do? What if they were humans acting out those..."

"That's the point. Human's can't. *Ersatzes* can!"

"And what if they feel the same as you and I? What if they.... The very idea is sickening. That is sinful! Terrible!" Claire cried, on the verge of tears. "Something has happened...to me...Eddy. Ever since the story broke today I can't get it out of my mind!"

"You were always soft," he pointed out, a little less accusing than he might have been a couple of days before.

"But this is different!" she exclaimed.

After a moment he nodded. "It got to me, too."

Silence, long and awkward, and then Claire's expression changed. "You do act different! You see it my way, don't you?"

"A little, maybe," he admitted, remembering the sick feeling he'd experienced at the end of the ballet.

"Then you'll do something?"

"Anything I can—but I just can't do anything, Claire. You know that!"

"I believe you could." She was thoughtful for some moments, then suggested: "Why not a campaign to 'humanize' Benny. It would make wonderful press. Just think what the mothers...well, every mother would be thinking about her own children, and that would surely help the case for Benny and..."

"Please, Claire..." He put a finger on her full, red lips. They stared at one another for a few seconds and then he laughed. "Okay—okay, I guess you have something there, after all!"

Just then the ground-car slipped up a ramp, speeding two roadway levels higher and then shot into the arched entrance to the *Stellar Hotel.*

* * * * * * *

Mr. Smithington Adams came home, curious and sick inside. He had been in the Social Police Headquarters for the most part of the day. The moment he walked into their small, old house and saw the newly delivered *ersatz* that had been sent by *Ersatz Inc.,* the fury built in him.

The day had been most frustrating to him. First Benny's escape and then all the fuss being made over it. Reporters had flocked to him, to get the story about the escape. Then there had been that Edmund Canfield from the *National Star,* with Mr. Ken Brown, pushing to get legal possession of Benny. That was most frustrating, because he could use the money such a deal would make. But some high official, who had remained nameless, had instructed him at Police Headquarters not to do anything—that he was not to sell Benny.

He glared at the *ersatz,* which stood in the corner of the room looking back with a bland expression on its face.

"You blasted creatures!" Adams cursed, stepping forward and hitting the *ersatz* in the face. "Why the hell would one of you run away?"

The *ersatz*'s face showed quick fear; it backed away, frightened.

"Answer me!" Adams demanded, hitting it in

the stomach.

His wife walked into the room.

"What are you doing?" she asked in a disinterested voice.

"Shut up!" Adams cried, hitting the *ersatz* and feeling a sense of satisfaction as the creature doubled up, moaning in "*ersatz*" anguish.

Adams kicked the *ersatz* one more time the way he wanted to kick his wife—just because of the way life had been for them for so long.

He looked at his wife, tried to remember what it had been like to desire her; what it had been like when they had found love and pleasure in each other's arms. But he couldn't remember because it had been too long a time.

One more kick at the *ersatz* caused it to double over and sink to the floor, writhing in agony.

"Let's eat!" Adams said to his wife, turning and not even paying any attention to the groaning *ersatz*.

* * * * * * *

The next morning J. B. Harrington was nursing a light hangover. The woman lying next to him on the bed was a fiery ball of energy which had drained him the evening before. He turned, looked at her.

Lovely Ann Laymont. He had met her several times in the past, but this was the first time he'd taken her to his home, the first time they had spent the night together in the same bed.

She was lying on top of the blankets. The slow, light breathing moved her breasts, and he slipped closer and tenderly kissed her lips.

Her eyes opened.

"Jay—you darling," she murmured. They kissed and then he felt her slip closer. "I'm so glad you invited me," she announced softly in his ear. "I've had a thing for you for a long time."

She trembled slightly. "You're quite a man!"

Harrington laughed; it was a low, barrel-chested laugh. "We make one hell of a pair. You, tiny, me big and-"

"Strong!" she told him, patting his cheek. "I never enjoyed anything so much. Who would have guessed that the great Harrington would be as good a lover as he is a lawyer?"

Just as his lips were moving down her shoulder, a buzzing sounded from the telescreen on the far wall.

He decided to ignore it. Then as it continued he angrily got up, went to the screen, activated it and found himself looking into the features of Ken Brown.

"What the hell do you want this time in the morning!" he exploded angrily.

Brown grinned. "It's eleven! I tried to get you at the office, but got switched. Sorry if I bothered you."

Harrington sighed. "What is it?" But he already had guessed.

"I have to see you, Jay. It's important and private." The implication in his voice assured Harrington what it was about.

"What's gotten into you, John?" Harrington exploded. "You mess with this *ersatz* thing much longer and you'll find yourself in a holy mess up to your neck! Literally holy! Confess your sins!"

"As a friend?" Brown almost pleaded.

"Hell!" Harrington thought for a moment and then said: "Okay, come over to the apartment about—make it noon time!"

With that, Harrington killed the connection and turned, looked at Ann Laymont.

Her black hair was flowing over her naked shoulders, making the flesh seem even whiter than it already was. She looked lovely.

He remembered all the times he had seen her at parties, how many times he had wondered what it might be like to make love to her. They had talked, carried on intelligent legal conversations, but never anything intimate, until the night before. It was at the bar and both of them were trying out Palmer's new discovery—the Martini. That had done it.

Ann Laymont worked for another lawyer in another section of town, and they had never had a chance to meet professionally, since each firm specialized in different branches of law. The Blanchard firm was a corporation law office, while Harrington was more concerned with criminal law; a branch that was restricted and not too popular with lawyers, though quite popular with the press and public. Harrington had made himself a reputation with the public as a lawyer who never lost.

Ann sat up in bed, asked: "He's going to ask you to take his case about this...Benny? Isn't he?"

Harrington grunted, flicked a wall switch and picked up the cigar which offered itself to him. He sat down on the bed next to Ann.

"Are you going to take it?" she asked.

"Hell! He hasn't asked me!"

"You will take it, won't you?" she pushed in an excited voice.

"Hell! I don't know anything other than what I've seen in the media. You know no respectable lawyer forms any personal opinions from what he reads."

"But you'll take it, won't you—because he's a friend. I've heard about you...and your *friends*," she said in an accusing voice.

"I don't know anything about the *ersatz* situation in general. It's really out of my line! So..."

Ann reached out and touched his shoulder. "If anybody could win—you could," she said in a voice filled with admiration.

"You certainly talk me up! Considering you don't even work for me!" he laughed.

"I've always wanted to."

"You're hired!" he laughed.

She was serious. "I meant it."

"Why not? I could use somebody like you at the office. We're overloaded and—hey, what am I saying?" He studied her, seriously, for a moment. "I shouldn't be doing this—but would you really consider it?"

"At the snap of an exploding rocket!" she cried. "I'd *love* to!"

"Okay—you're hired! As of now!"

"I couldn't!"

"Okay—I know about the two week notice and all that, but you can help me out. This is Saturday...so I work Saturdays, too, it looks like!" His voice faded out as he looked at her beautiful body. "I never have mixed business with pleasure before...I just hope this won't get in the way of what we were doing!"

"Loving?" she laughed, coming into his arms.

"Why should it?"

Their lips met, and they tensed together.

He thought: *She's one hell of a good looking woman for thirty-five! One hell of a good looker!*

Later, as he lay exhaustedly next to Ann, his thoughts turned inward, considering the woman beside him and his long, lonely life which had stretched out for well over forty years.

After high school there had been the stretch in the redefined Peace Corps and then he'd gone to college, taken up law, and fallen in love with a lovely, dark haired girl a couple of years younger than himself. As he remembered Joan Sherman, he suddenly realized how much Ann was like her. Maybe that had been the reason for his quick, abrupt liking for Ann. His romance and affair with Joan had continued through the six years in college. Then, a couple of months before they were to be married, she was killed in the '57 highway breakdown that had startled the nation and forced a new law which demanded more safety measures in the automatic highway systems. The shock of her death had driven his head into the law books, and he'd continued to study for another three years, without even looking at any women. It wasn't for another five years that he became involved in an affair with a young woman his own age. That had lasted a little over two years and folded. From the beginning he had been sure it would never last—even though they had talked about marriage. He hadn't been able to forget Joan. A lot of years had gone by since then. He turned, stared at Ann Laymont, now fully realizing his attraction for her. Maybe this would be the woman who could develop into something—more lasting, more serious. Harrington realized that he was getting to the age where he either got married, had a child fast, or had to forget the whole thing.

The apartment door buzzer rang at that point and Harrington jerked, as if shot. For a moment he couldn't imagine who it was. Then he remembered about Brown's call.

"Here it comes!" he sighed, pushing his heavy weight up from the bed and standing. He looked down at Ann, made a face, and then raised his shoulders in a helpless gesture.

"You'll help him?" Ann asked.

"Fiends! Damn them!" With that, Harrington stooped over, pressed the front door release, which was located on the bed stand, said: "Come on in, Brown. I'll be right out."

Then to Ann, he said: "Stay here…listen, take notes if you need to. I want to know what you think…"

* * * * * * *

J. B. Harrington glared at Brown, his lips working nervously on the cigar, moving it from one side of his mouth to the other.

They were sitting in the lounge room, a small but cozy place. He'd dialed for two chairs, a coffee table and a couple of drinks.

Ann was listening in the bedroom. He hadn't mentioned her to Brown. She could hear what was said.

Harrington leaned forward, resting his weight on his knees. "Okay—so you insist on pushing this— matter. You want the *ersatz* named Benny. Okay.

Why?" His small eyes narrowed and he snapped the cigar from his heavy lips, pointing it at the other man.

"Why?" Brown countered carefully, "I can't quite understand it myself. I've given it a lot of thought, believe me. All night. Everything has happened point by point—adding up to my being here, now. My daughter was saved by the *ersatz*—it was her birthday, you know, and she wanted to have Benny for herself.

"Now, suddenly that doesn't seem to be the point at all. It's gone beyond that. At first I didn't think it would be so complicated. Just go to the owner, give him several hundred dollars and then be finished. Now things have progressed beyond that."

"You can say that again!" Harrington exploded.

"After getting the restraining order I thought that would be the end of it. But Adams is a small, vengeful man. A real bastard!" he said with some heat, his face hardening, and his eyes becoming narrow slits of anger. "As far as he's concerned the matter is a closed issue. He wants the *ersatz* disposed of. That just doesn't seem right.

"I don't know why it means so damned much to me now, except, no matter what, I want to fight.

"Now it's become a point of principle. A matter of ethics. Let's say a form of reward. Or maybe mere curiosity.

"Why did the *ersatz* run away? Terror? Fear of being killed? That means they have a survival instinct. Why did it try to save Jeannie? Surely the survival instinct would have made it realize that such an act would reveal its identity. Yet it risked everything to save my little girl. I don't think it's a mindless thing. For the first time in my life I begin to wonder exactly *what* it must be like to be an *ersatz* what it might be like to be a synman, beaten, killed...depending on what my Master desired to do to me. I've looked into the matter since the incident—learned a few things.

"*Ersatzes* are given emotions—so that terror and fear will reflect in their reactions and expression while being knocked around. If they have emotions, maybe they have—well, soul isn't the right thing—but they have a *personality* of sorts. A personality that seeks and desires life. Am I making sense?"

Harrington chewed on his cigar, running the man's words through his mind.

"Yes—I believe you make sense," he said slowly. Then stabbing the cigar at Brown, he added: "And I believe maybe it's about time to do something about the *ersatz* problem."

He stopped, amazed at his own words. "What the hell! You've got me talking like a fool, now!"

He was silent for a long time, thinking over what the man had just said. Maybe it made sense. Maybe not. But if it did....

That thought stuck in his mind, like a two-edged knife.

Harrington sighed. "You know, John, it isn't the first time an *ersatz* ran away. It won't be the last one. But maybe...if you were to fight this all the way to the bitter end."

The lawyer hesitated again, his mind suddenly excited at the challenge the issue presented to his legal knowledge. "You know—this could be a history making trial." He smiled, his face wrinkling. "A sensational one! A *real* challenge! And I've never had one exactly like this! A machine with a soul. Fantastic. Stupid. Impossible! Yet…who knows?"

Silence was heavy in the room. Then Harrington stood. "Are you really sure you want to go through with this? Once we start they're be no backing out. And the end results, regardless of what they might be will hang around our necks until the day we die!"

"I'm quite sure. No *personality* should go unrewarded for an act of sacrifice. Thinking being, human, or *ersatz*!"

"It's going to be messy, and it'll shake up everybody in the nation—the world—because it could, very well could, change the whole attitude toward man and God and *ersatzes*!" Harrington warned. "For merely a matter of principle it could be very, very messy. We already have overpopulation! Barely under control. And making a lot of *ersatzes*…equal to us…well…its gonna be a whooper!"

"It'll be worth it. Benny is the first *ersatz* to have done such a thing—I want him for Jeannie.

"I want him to watch over her—and if possible, I'll *have* him!"

* * * * * * *

REV. G. CLAY BELMONT TO ACT AS D.A. IN *ERSATZ* CASE

The learned and famous minister and lawyer, Rev. G. Clay Belmont, was named today as acting D.A. in the case involving the State vs. Brown, over the issue of the *ersatz* known as Benny. Rev. Belmont was interviewed in his Pennington Apartments in San Francisco today and had this short statement to make concerning his role in the *ersatz* case. "I don't know what Harrington might have in mind; but he's cooking up the wrong rocket fuel. It seems incredible to me that such a famous and learned lawyer would—even for personal friendship—enter such a childishly foolish case.

"The fact is: there *is* no case. Brown is merely making a lot of noise over nothing!"

When asked how long he expected the trial to last, he said: "Not more than a few minutes—at most. Once I've made my opening statement, I'm sure Harrington will advise a total, swift withdrawal."

Harrington was approached and told of Belmont's statements and he merely said: "If he thinks it's going to be an easy pushover, he's in for a surprise. It's about time something was done about this situation—and we plan on doing it."

He asked exactly what he meant by this, and said: "No comment. See you in court tomorrow!"

CHAPTER SIX

"All rise for the honorable Judge Thomas, Judge of the High Court of Records."

The large courtroom came to attention. The buzzing conversation which made the huge room like a living thing became dead. All eyes turned to the judge's box as the regal man stepped forward and seated himself.

Thomas looked old. The man's face was drained and tense, his shoulders stooped as if carrying too much weight. He sat there for a long time before speaking.

"We are gathered here to consider a Ruling on the case of Brown vs. the State. The issue is of such a dramatic consequence that our daily media have made undue publicity on its account. I want it put on record that this Court will not be influenced by the such public attention. The judgment that will be founded in these halls will be made purely on the legal arguments offered by the State Prosecutor, Rev. G. Clay Belmont, and Counsel for Brown, J. B. Harrington. The D.A. Office has allowed the services of Rev. Belmont because of his high regard and position in the Land to argue the case against Brown." Thomas paused and then nodded to Belmont. "The Court waits for your opening statement."

Belmont, a tall, white haired man with a hawk nose and eyes like black fire pools, stood, pushed back his black Court coat and then turned to the audience which was packed into the room, his eyes flicking to the telecams.

"That State claims that our Law reads simply, and that it cannot be twisted or turned upside down—"

"Objection," Harrington cried. "There is no indication that we wish to twist existing laws."

Judge Thomas snapped his eyes at Harrington and said: "You are out of order interrupting the reading of the charges."

"I object, your honor, merely to the statement that we are here to twist any existing laws. I feel that such a statement placed on the record might-"

"Objection overruled," the judge interrupted savagely, turning his attention to Belmont. "You may continue."

"As I was saying," Belmont said in his deep bass voice, projecting it over the full extent of the room so that everybody could easily hear his words, "the Law reads quite clearly on this issue. Quote: 'Any *ersatz* whosoever might run away, show signs of rebellion...etc...will be automatically disposed of.' Unquote. That we are here at all is a contradiction of the existing Law. What the Counsel wishes to prove by his insistence on this hearing is beyond my understanding and—"

"Objection. My honored friend here is already inserting personal opinion. This can be saved for his summation. It is completely out of place at this time."

"You need not remind the Court of the law. Restrict yourself merely to the charges, Rev. Belmont."

Belmont coughed and then after taking a deep breath continued: "Rather than bore the Court with the obvious facts of Law concerning *ersatzes*, I will satisfy the point by simplifying the complications into a few short paragraphs.

"First. *Ersatzes* were a development of Able Brothers, Inc. on contract of the World Council. It was ordered that a substitute man be created for the sole purpose of getting psychotic frustrations out of the systems of people who might, under other circumstances, commit crimes of violence.

"Overpopulation and crowded working and living conditions were the outgrowth of Universal Peace worked on the minds and emotions and nerves of the everyday man. Thus enforced birth control. Crime was becoming a common practice which couldn't be controlled. Doctors from all branches of science were gathered together to discuss the problem and it was discovered that under the strain of living in the complex of our society, people were striking out blindly for an outlet for their restrained emotions. The emotions had to have an outlet. Creativity wasn't enough. That had been tried from time to time, by letting people have more freedom from work. The three day week failed, creating larger crime waves. The Good Doctors decided the only solution was to cater to the pent-up emotions, to allow them free expression—not on humans, but on synthetic humans. Robots—*androids*. Robots were manufactured by the millions. People were required by Law to have at least one on which they could flood their inner fires, but that failed to completely solve the problem. It worked for a short while. Then it was discovered that these machines had no subconscious effect on the psychotic, and it was suggested by Able Brothers that the solution might be in a synman. An android who looked exactly like Man; so much like man that it was impossible to tell the difference. And *Ersatz, Inc.* became a national and then international success.

"The Bible said that we shall not kill. Man had dominion over the world and all that was in it. There was nothing against killing Man's creation. God could take the life of Man. Then it followed there was nothing against Man killing his own image and likeness. And what happened?"

Belmont's voice raised higher, his arms flying outwards to the audience. "Is there any crime?" He paused. "Is there any murder?"

He let silence answer him for a brief moment and then exclaimed, *"Why No! Of course not.* To think otherwise is a perversion, a sick distortion of Truth as any normal mind of man will automatically realize!

"All the problems which plagued man—and all the inner frustrations that had caused him to war upon himself, have been finally eliminated. Terrorism is not only outlawed, but unnecessary in a world of universal peace! There is no crime. There is no war. There is Happiness. Happiness all the time. We have everything. Anything we want. We even have our *ersatzes*—made in our images for the sole purpose of curing all inner antagonism, hate, frustration. And what a gift to Humankind! What a wonderful invention of our creative and scientific minds—what a wonderful solution to all the problems of our world!

"And now—*now* we have this man, this man named Brown, who wishes to give *ersatzes*—our creations, nothing but synthetic men of synflesh and steel—the right to the same considerations as *humans*. This is madness. Beyond madness. It is sick! Disgusting! It is…"

"Objection. He's inserting his personal bias!"

"Never mind that. Objection overruled!" The judge nodded to the man. "Continue. But you can keep it a bit less verbose, please!"

Belmont shrugged, as if feeling helpless, but smiled for the world wide audience: "Do we forgive a washer when it doesn't work?

"No!

"We junk it—get a new one.

"Do we feel sorry when our car doesn't work? Try to give it forgiveness—to have it used again?

"No! It's a sin to repair the old. Take a *new* one. That's what they're there for.

"What is the issue here? Really? What are we here for?

"Because one man has decided that an *ersatz* deserves to live. To live. Consider that. The assumption is that a machine is alive!"

"Objection. It is *obviously* alive. At least that's the core of the issues—"

Loud laughter came from the audience and the judge pounded his gavel. "We'll have none of that! Objection denied. Regardless of your reasons! Mr. Belmont please do continue."

"Yes. As I was saying…. The assumption is that

a machine is alive! But what do we really have here? A machine malfunction and nothing more. Simply put: we have an *ersatz* which has rebelled against its creator. Dared to act as if it had a mind of its own—and most importantly, as if it were equal to its master and creator! That's as if we were to rebel against our Creator! And we all know what the Good Book says about that subject!"

Belmont paused, dramatically. "This has nothing to do with personalities—who ever considered a washing machine with personality? Well, okay, we sometimes allude to our possessions as if they were...well, personalities, even giving them pet names. But that's a game! And nobody is deluded into thinking it has any true meaning—it is not suggesting that Lenny the Family Car is really something alive and with an actual personality or soul!"

The man paused again. Throwing his large hands in the air, arms seeming to embrace the whole world. "Malfunctioning. That's the word we must keep in mind!"

He slammed a fist into his hand, causing a loud smack sound to drive home his point.

"We don't use a dishwasher that is not working right. Get a new one.

"What is so special about this *ersatz* that a Citizen should cry for such a *machine's* 'life?' What—"

"Objected to," Harrington exclaimed, standing. Judge Thomas raised an eyebrow, puzzled.

"What objection now?"

"To the term 'machine' in reference to *ersatz*—in particular to the specific one by the name of Benny."

A roar of disapproval exploded from the audience. It was several minutes before the judge could calm them. He hammered the gavel several times after silence had finally settled in the courtroom.

"Any more outbursts like that and I'll clear the court." Turning his eyes toward Harrington, he said: "What possible objection? *Ersatzes are* machines. There is no question or issue about this fact."

"I object because this is the very issue here. This is what the case for the defense wishes to bring out."

A murmur sounded from the audience. The shouts of indignation came from several voices. Thomas moved the gavel up and down and once silence had returned, looked probingly at Harrington. It was a long time before he spoke.

"I don't know what you have in mind, Counsel, but I can assure you the Court looks upon it with more than just horrified puzzlement." The emotion that was caught up in his voice made it impossible for him to continue. After a moment he said: "However, since it is a minor point at this time, I'll advise Rev. Belmont to refrain from referring to...'Benny'...as a machine. It is enough to use the term *ersatz*."

Belmont turned savagely toward Harrington.

"You mean to imply that you believe that *ersatzes* have Souls like Man? That they are—"

"I imply nothing of the kind," Harrington interrupted. "Merely that the term 'machine' is objectionable under the circumstances, which my defense will prove in due time—when you have tired of your oratory and given me a chance to make my opening statement."

Belmont's face turned purple and the cords of his thin neck knotted. He was about to say something when Judge Thomas broke in.

"We will have no private arguments between the two Counsels. Your remark, Mr. Harrington, was completely out of order, and let me warn you that another such statement will place you in contempt of Court." He nodded to Belmont to continue.

"What I was beginning to say was that it seemed impossible to conceive that a Citizen would attempt to protect the rights of a...an *ersatz*.

"But now it would seem that they wish to suggest that *ersatzes* are something more than machines-"

"Objected to."

"You will rephrase your statement, Rev. Belmont."

"Are other than mere mechanical toys created by—"

"Objected to."

"Now Mr. Harrington, I believe you are pushing your point too far. Rev. Belmont has every right to refer to *ersatzes* as mechanical devices."

"Objected to on the grounds that it is a leading statement which I wish not put into the record. I want the *Grand Jury Brain* to consider the facts—"

"For Heaven's sake!" Belmont exploded. "The facts are simply that we created them. They are mechanical devices and—"

"They are, I'll admit, creations of man, but that they are *merely* mechanical devices is the issue that I will be putting to the Court. The whole point of the case is based on my own personal conviction, supported by the action of Benny, that *ersatzes* are more than mere robotic devices in the shape of man, but are actually the most wonderful, ingenious crea-

100

tion that man has ever created. I contend that they are—"

"Mr. Harrington, you'll have your chance to make your opening statement *after* Rev. Belmont has concluded. We would like to take things in an orderly fashion." He looked at Belmont and said:

"You will please refrain from the use of me-chanical devices or any term there such."

"If I'm not allowed to define my point, then I'll be concluding with the following:

"I wish one point kept in mind: *ersatzes* are creations—like any other creations-"

"Objected to."

"Never mind. I'll rephrase. They are creations much like other creations of man. Created in man's mind for a simple purpose of being used as he sees fit. There are certain rules and laws governing *ersatzes* which state that if these rules are broken, then the creation is done away with—replaced by a new one—one which is unfaulty."

"Objection. I resent the term unfaulty; it leads to the conclusion that there is something wrong with Benny. There is nothing wrong with Benny—in fact I wish to prove there is something exceptional about him."

Judge Thomas sighed and then closed his eyes. After a moment he looked at Belmont and said:

"Objection sustained."

"*I* object to the Counsel continuing to confuse the case by side issues. I object to any implications that *ersatzes* are anything different than the law reads them to be—than the creators meant them to be! That's an outrage!"

"Your objection is well taken, but considering

that Citizen Brown has the right by Sec 5, Para G3 of the World Citizens Rights—to quote: 'To bring to issue any point he so wishes, regardless of public or legal consideration, sane or insane, before a High Court of Records to be judged'...etc. unquote—I'll have to sustain the objection."

After taking several heavy breaths, Belmont looked helplessly at the audience and then into the telecams. "Under the circumstances all that I can do is to rest my opening statement." He turned and sat at the State bench.

Judge Thomas nodded to Harrington. "You may make your opening statement now."

Harrington stood, his huge bulk impressive. He ignored the audience and the cameras, directing his remarks to Judge Thomas.

"I will be brief—unlike my learned opponent." He let silence settle over the courtroom and then began.

"We wish to contend that while *ersatzes* were created for the sole purpose of giving humans an outlet for their anxieties and frustrations, that they have turned out—like many inventions of man—to be more than what the inventor meant them to be. And, unlike other inventions, they are our most gloriously wonderful creations, and should be treated as such. To compare them to washing machines, to robots, or cars, is, we contend, like comparing the discovery of atomic rockets to fire crackers.

"It is not to suggest that *ersatzes* have the Divine spark of a Soul—for only God can give a Soul to a creation—but rather to suggest that possibly in this fine creation we have brought upon the world is a living thing that has every property of man—

except a Divine Soul.

"It will be in our argument that there is a difference between a Divine Soul and the *personality quota* which is possessed by *ersatzes*.

"After all, we find nothing wrong with rewarding a dog for a good deed—or for performing a cute trick. And the Bible, as my learned opponent will admit, suggests that only man has a Soul.

"It would be out of place here to say that *ersatzes* can even be compared to having the same kind of life as a dog—for surely God gave even such a low creature as the ant a Divine spark of life.

"It is not our intention to compare *ersatzes* to anything which God created. In fact, this is the very contention of our case.

"An *ersatz* should *not* be compared to creations of God, or other creations of man.

"We contend that *ersatzes* are unique. They defy comparison. They defy classification. They are in a category all their own—and it's about time that something was done to point this out.

"This is why we are here today. This is why we should be here.

"And we are here to prove that *ersatzes* deserve a different place in our minds and in our laws.

"And, furthermore, we contend that what applies to all *ersatzes* does not necessarily apply to Benny.

"Who's to say that something might not have been different in the creation of Benny? Something which gave him a sense of values?

"We will prove beyond all doubt that Benny, at least, deserves special consideration for his act of sacrifice."

Harrington turned and walked to his seat.

CHAPTER SEVEN

Silence filled the room like an angry, seething thing and wasn't broken for several moments.

"Reverend Belmont," the judge said, "you may bring your first witness."

"Call David Carlton to the stand."

A young, eager-eyed man came forward, was sworn in and then sat in the witness box.

"Your name and occupation?" Belmont asked.

"David Carlton, medico for the Los Angeles Medi-Corps."

"Do you remember the date of June 7 of this year? Did anything special happen?"

"Yes. I was called to the scene of an accident. A car had knocked over an *ersatz* but I hadn't been informed it was an *ersatz*."

"Was there anything different about this *ersatz*?"

"Only that his legs had been damaged."

"That is all." Belmont returned to his bench.

Harrington stood, approached the medico and then, smiling, said: "You look like a bright young man. I guess you've had an excellent training in medical school."

Carlton grinned. "Went to Davis-Davis and Temple."

"Got degrees?"

"Yes. Master's."

"I understand that these schools are specifically for the treatment of humans? I'm right about that?" His voice was oiled in friendliness.

"That is correct."

"Then you're not an expert on *ersatzes*!" Harrington spat savagely at the young man.

Carlton shuffled in his seat. His face reddened. "No—I can't say I am—but what's there to know?"

"I'm finished with this witness."

The young man stepped down as Belmont called: "Maple Edgerton."

A matronly woman stepped forward, was sworn and then settled into the witness box.

"I understand that you witnessed the accident on June 7th?"

"I saw it all. The *ersatz* ran across the street and saved the girl's life."

"Do you believe that there was anything unusual about this action—"

"Objected to, since it calls for an opinion."

Judge Thomas stared at Harrington. "I should think that you would desire such a question to be entered onto the record."

"I am not interested in opinions of laymen on *ersatzes*. In fact, to be honest, I'm surprised that the Counsel for State has called these two people, for it would seem against his own interest."

The judge nodded agreement.

Belmont smiled, said: "I only wish to bring into evidence the facts in this case. This is the only way possible. I assure you that I'm well aware of the danger here—but it is also not my contention to

106

suggest that the facts did not happen. I only wish to let the Court examine them, honestly, and then see that even under such circumstances there is no call for special consideration. As my case continues, what I'm leading up to will become clear. I would like the witness to answer the question."

The judge considered and then said: "Since it is to the benefit of the defense, I can see no possible reason that her personal opinion not be recorded here, but as the opinion of a layman. The objection is overruled."

"Answer the question. What was your reaction? Did you think there was anything unusual about the incident?" Belmont asked.

The woman beamed and then said: "There surely was something unusual. I've tried to figure it out—it seems impossible that an *ersatz* would act in this manner. It's unheard of."

"Objection! Since the witness is not an authority on the subject of what *ersatzes* do or don't do, her experience would be obviously limited."

"Sustained."

"That is all." Belmont sat.

Harrington stood, looked at the witness.

"Well, Mrs. Edgerton, tell me, how many *ersatzes* have you had in your life?"

"Oh, I guess...let me see." She, mentally counted and then said: "Seventeen."

"How many were you personally responsible for killing?"

Her face beamed happily. "Why at least twelve—no—maybe thirteen."

"How many times have you beaten an *ersatz*?"

"Oh, many. Many. I don't know. It is such a

wonderful thing...and I've...well...enjoyed the benefits. You know."

"Yes. Yes. I quite imagine! Would you say that the *ersatz* Benny deserved any special consideration?"

"Why? It's just an *ersatz*!"

"Then you are obviously prejudiced about the place of *ersatzes* in society."

Amazement flowered her features. "Why they have only one place. And I just *love* it! There is no question about what they're here for."

"And what is this place?"

"To...to...well, they are...there is...a...they were made to serve man.

"Thank you. That is all." Harrington was smiling as he sat down.

"I wish a redirect," Belmont stood. "Tell me what you mean by to serve man.

Maple Edgerton showed relief in her face. "Well they are here for us to use any way we see fit."

"Thank you."

"Redirect," Harrington exclaimed, standing.

"Tell me, do you have a pet?"

"Naturally! Of course!" she beamed as if relieved that he hadn't continued on the same level of questioning.

"Do you love your pet?"

"Of course, the little darling—why the other day-"

"We aren't interested in the *other day*. Please just answer the questions." Harrington hesitated and then turned his back to the witness.

"Now tell me, do you reward your pet?"

"I don't understand the question."

"Do you show it affection—do *you* feed it well, do you take care of it, are you kind to it?"

"Of course. *Bettie* is a wonderful dog."

"Then you must reward it for being good."

"Yes."

"Can it talk?"

"Of course not. No dog can talk. Why are you being so silly?"

"Can it do things around the house for you?"

"Of course not. Not supposed to!"

"Yet you show love and affection and reward to something which only shows a responding love and affection to you. Is that right?"

"Yes." She looked down, moving nervously.

"Yet to something which can communicate to you, could do work for you, and could possibly show an act of mercy –"

"Objected to," Belmont cried, standing. "That is an assumption, not a proven fact."

"Sustained."

"Then I'll reword it. Tell me, if you had Benny—who we know is quite able to do an act of self-sacrifice—would you reward it?"

The response was filled with loathing and disgust: "An *ersatz*?"

"That's all I want to know. I'm through with this witness!" Harrington walked to his bench, contempt showing on his face.

* * * * * * *

"Call Dr. Norton to the stand," Belmont ordered.

When he had been sworn, Belmont stood and

walked to the small, thin, gray haired man. "Tell me, Doctor, what is your profession?"

"I'm a doctor of *Ersatz* Medicine.*"

"Could you please give us your background?" During the next minutes Dr. Norton listed his medical background, indicated that he had worked with *Ersatz Inc.* for fifteen years and before that had been highly responsible for some of the development which had helped to perfect the *ersatz* to its present level.

"Now, tell me, Dr. Norton, have you any knowledge of the *ersatz* B-797868420T03?"

"At your request some days ago I checked the files on this particular *ersatz*."

"Could you tell the Court exactly what your findings were?"

"That there was nothing unusual about this particular one. That nothing went wrong—that it came off the assembly line exactly like all other *ersatzes*."

"In your considered *expert* opinion, could you tell me exactly what makes up the mental processes of the *ersatz* mind?"

"To use the term 'mind' is quite an error. For an *ersatz* has merely a functioning—let's call it conditioned responses—"

"Objection."

"For heaven's sake—does the Counsel for the defense wish to argue the terms used by such a man as Dr. Norton?" Belmont exploded.

Judge Thomas turned serious eyes toward Harrington.

"The objection is your Honor, concerning the words 'conditioned responses.' It suggests no freedom of action. The facts of this case, which have already been brought to the attention of the Court, are that this is not true. Benny did do something which involved a freedom of choice and-"

"May I interrupt, sir," Dr. Norton broke in.

Judge Thomas snapped his eyes at the witness. "This is quite out of order—but if you have something to say pertaining to the objection I will allow a short statement."

"It does. My term 'conditioned response' might well be poorly chosen. As Mr. Harrington pointed out, it is limiting the scope of possibilities of the *ersatz*. Maybe I should have said that there is a certain amount of conditioned response placed in the control center of the *ersatz* 'brain'—this response includes many complications and does give a close semblance to free choice and thought—if one wishes to look at it in this way. I was only attempting to simplify the terminology."

"I withdraw the objection under consideration because of what the doctor has now said," Harrington announced. The expression on his face revealed pleasure.

Belmont glared first at Harrington and then at his own witness.

"Doctor, are you to lead us to believe that the *ersatz* has reasoning powers—a freedom of choice and can—like humans—make rational decisions?"

"Nothing of the kind. Merely that we have conditioned the brain centers to respond as nearly as possible like the human brain—in order to lend a more human *emotional* response."

Belmont smiled and then asked: "Could you explain this?"

"Well, to begin with, one has to consider the

reasoning behind the development of the *ersatz*. The *ersatz* was created as a substitute for murder and violence. It is something more than a robot. It was necessary to create an android that could react when being beaten—when being killed. It had to have emotional reflex actions. Even the so called 'blood' was colored red to have the appearance of human blood. The skin was made to look like human skin; to break and cut and bleed. Syn-muscles were created that could be torn and ripped. The only difference is that the *ersatz* can take more punishment than a human being—which has the advantage that it gives the owner more emotional satisfaction. The longer it takes to kill the *ersatz*, the longer the torture—or beating—the more the human master could release his emotional tensions. The cowering *ersatz*, crying, screaming, moaning out its agony gives all the outward signs a human would give. In fact there is more psychological release in seeing an *ersatz* dying before your eyes than watching a human being doing the same thing. The psychological release is complete—far beyond that necessary to burn out the fury and frustration which bothers the individual involved."

"Could you go into the mental processes of the *ersatz*?"

"All we can do is to make an educated guess, not being *ersatz* ourselves. It is accepted among authorities that the *ersatz* is synthetic, and so are the emotional responses. They have built-in conditioning. We create a—well it's like programming an M-Brain. You feed information into the Brain—facts and data. With the *ersatz* we graph emotional information from many human sources, and then they are fed into the newly formed brain syn-cells."

"Then you might say—if I understand you right—that the *ersatz* is merely a complicated recording of human emotions? A reflection—without any personality of its own?"

"I would say that's a fairly close-"

"Yes or no?" Belmont interrupted, driving his point into the Doctor's face with a gnarled finger.

"Well—yes."

"That'll be all. Thank you, Doctor."

Harrington stood, faced the witness and then slowly asked: "You weren't quite sure about that statement, were you doctor?"

"Which one?"

"The summation that my learned opponent made of your explanation about the *ersatz*'s personality quota."

"Well, you see, it's because there are other opinions and no clear cut way of proving *any* of them."

"Could you tell us some of the other opinions which make you hesitate?"

Belmont stood: "I object to that question since it calls for hearsay information—not concerning the doctor's own personal opinion. It is immaterial—and if the Counsel wishes such opinions he can bring his own witnesses to the stand."

Judge Thomas said: "Considering that it can be merely stated as scientific theory—acceptable to other authorities on the subject, I believe there's no reason not to let Dr. Norton relate what he has read on the subject, since it seems to contribute to his reluctance to make a clear-cut statement of his own. I believe Mr. Harrington is merely attempting to clarify the doctor's own opinion, which you tried to establish. As an authority on the subject he has every right to show all sides of the issue—as he sees them.

"I will allow the question. You will answer it, Doctor."

"One opinion which I clearly disagree with is that an *ersatz* has the ability to think as we do. Some radical schools of thought make that contention. To think for yourself is to do more than react to stimuli. My personal belief is that the *ersatz* react to stimuli. Things which take place around it and things which are said to it or that it hears. This does not mean that it has an emotional reaction like a human—like the ability to cry from an emotional hurt. Simply that there *is* a reaction."

"Would you say that it has a personality of its own?"

"That depends on what you call a personality. What makes personality? Environment, things that happen around a person and—"

Belmont cried: "I object to that statement on the grounds that it implies an *ersatz* can be equated to a person."

"The objection is well stated."

"Your Honor," Dr. Norton said, turning his eyes up to the judge. "I only meant this as an explanation—I meant in no way to equate an *ersatz* to a human. *This is quite impossible!* All scientists agree, one might say, that what takes place around a human help to develop them and thus, one could say: makes up his personality. Experience makes us what we are as human beings. We experience life. We change. We learn and become better people."

Judge Thomas looked at Belmont, but no objection was made. "You may continue."

114

"You were talking about the personality of—or rather the possible personality of an *ersatz*," Harrington reminded.

"Yes. To the extent that an *ersatz* has a surrounding environment one would have to conclude that it would *learn* to respond to the stimulus of his environment."

"Then you are saying that one *ersatz* can be different from another."

Dr. Norton hesitated, looking at Belmont.

"Answer the question, please."

Belmont stood, alarm distorting his thin features. "I'll object to that since it calls for a conclusion which the witness admittedly claimed would be impossible to know. He implied that there were areas which it was impossible to *know*. That only an *ersatz* might know—" Belmont broke off, his face flushing. Angrily he sat 'I withdraw the objection."

Harrington grinned, pleased at the trap Belmont had fallen into.

"As you were saying?" Harrington said. "One *ersatz*, in your considered, expert opinion, could possibly be different from another *ersatz* because of its environment. Yes or no?"

"It is possible."

"That is all. Redirect?" The last word was directed snidely to Belmont, who silently fumed in his seat, shaking his head.

"You may step down," Judge Thomas said to the Doctor.

"Call Dr. Jefferson to the stand," Belmont said.

Jefferson was an elderly man with shock white hair, his pudgy face was beet red and his large eyes had a fanatical gleam in them as he was sworn in.

"You are, am I right, a Minister of the Holy Church of God?" Belmont asked.

"Yes."

"Now what I've called on you for is your expert opinion on Man and on all of God's creatures."

"They are Divine. Of course! They have the Spark of Life. Of course. And man has the Soul. Of course!"

"And what does the Bible say in accordance to Man's place in the world?"

> *"God created man in his own image, in the image of God he created him; male and female he created them.*
>
> *"And God blessed them, and God said to them, Be fruitful, and multiply, and fill the earth, and subdue it; and have dominion over the fish of the sea, and over the fowl of the air, and over the cattle, and over all the wild beasts that move upon the earth."*

"That would include *all* things on the earth?"

"That is what God said. Of course!"

"Would that include all of Man's creations?"

"That's what the Good Book meant," the man grinned. "Of course!"

"And would that include such a creation as the *ersatz*?"

"It would."

"In your considered opinion, what is an *ersatz?*"

"Objected to on the grounds he is not an expert on *ersatzes.*"

"Considering that he *is* an expert on Man and

116

God and that he is only expressing the place that the Church would put on it, I object to the objection," Belmont exclaimed.

"Objection overruled."

When everybody looked puzzled, the judge offered: "The *first* objection is overruled! *Mr. Harrington's* objection, that is! You may answer the question."

"*Ersatzes* are merely a synthetic device created for a single purpose, without Soul and without God's Divine spark. The *ersatz* is considered—by the Church—to be lower than all the fishes and all the fowl and all the creeping creatures on the earth. He is made of the clay of the earth by man—and he is lower than the clay. The Church considered that the *ersatz* is merely a mechanical—"

"Objection on the grounds that the Court already ruled on the term in reference to *ersatzes*."

Belmont glared at Harrington and then exploded: "He is giving the Church's dissertation on the *ersatz*. He is making no revelations. He is merely quoting Church policy."

"Still, I object!"

"Object all you like, but... *Objection overruled*."

"Continue," Belmont urged, grinning.

"The Church considers the *ersatz* a mechanical creation as it would consider the washing machine."

"Thank you, Doctor. That is all."

Harrington stood, approached the witness and then, smiling, said: "Tell me, is there any record—ruling in the Church records—considering the policy on washing machines?"

"Of course not."

"Then there is no official statement concerning washing machines?"

The witness shuffled nervously, looking at Belmont. Then said: "Well...it's not the way you—"

"Answer the question. Yes or no?"

"Well, no. If you insist on putting it that way!"

"I insist. Quite insist!"

"Well, then...no!"

"Is there any ruling on *any* device created by man?"

"No," Dr. Jefferson mumbled softly, his face whitening.

"Will you speak up so the Court can hear you?

"No," the witness blurted out savagely. "No! No! No!"

"Is there any official Church record concerning the *ersatz*?"

Dr. Jefferson glared at the lawyer, his lips white-rimmed, his eyes blazing hate.

"Go ahead, answer the question. Is there *any* mention of the *ersatz* in the Church record?"

"No. No! *No!* Of course not!"

"Objected to!" Harrington snapped.

The judge sighed: "It is your question! His answer. What can...oh, forget it. Objection overruled! He can...must continue!"

"Well...it's a damned bloody machine! We don't list official statements of policy concerning machines. The Church is only concerned with Man and God and the Soul—not with machines."

"Thank *you,* Dr. Jefferson."

A snicker sounded from the audience.

"Now tell me—since there is no written *official* records of the Church's opinion on *ersatzes*, how is it that you can state the Church believes the *ersatz* to have no Soul—to have no thoughts, to be lower than a dog, or a fish or a bird—or the earth itself? How is it that you can make these statements? And to assume that you are in a position to speak for the Church—make policy opinions for the Church?"

"Your honor," Belmont yelled. smashing his hand down hard against the State's bench. "I object violently to the defense badgering the witness—I object to his twisting the facts—to twisting the learned and honorable minister—to insulting him and his position in the Church. There is no call for such—such attitudes—such sinful twisting of the words of a man of God~"

"I can understand your objection—but the Counsel's point is well taken. Objection denied."

Harrington said: "I'm through with this witness!" His face was contemptuous as he turned toward the telecams.

"Doctor Jefferson," Belmont said, standing, "when you were making your statement considering Church policy about the *ersatzes*, were you actually making the point that such matters were below the consideration of the Church on the grounds that it was an obvious fact?"

Jefferson sighed out his relief. "Yes."

"Thank you."

Harrington stood, firing his question quickly at the Doctor. "Are you an expert on mechanical devices?"

"Well, no."

"Are you an expert on *ersatzes*?"

"No."

"Therefore, how can you have an opinion as to

their rightful place in the scale of things?"

"It's obvious—isn't it?"

"What's obvious? That *ersatzes* are merely mechanical devices?"

"Objected to since the defense counsel has already had a ruling made on the term mechanical." Belmont grinned triumphantly.

Judge Thomas smiled. "He's quite right."

"Then I'll reword. That *ersatzes* are below man? That they are to be compared to man? That they are something like man, but not man? What is it that is so obvious?"

Jefferson looked momentarily speechless and then he stood, hate burning like fire in his eyes. "It's obvious that they are nothing but machines."

"I move that be stricken from the record," Harrington demanded.

"It shall be stricken."

"But, your honor—they are *not* animals, they are mechanical devices!"

Judge Thomas banged his gavel and said: "The witness will refrain from making any more outbursts. Just answer the questions."

Jefferson slammed back down into his seat.

"The Church—from your own testimony," Harrington stated, "has no official policy concerning *ersatzes*. Is that right?"

"It needs no official—"

"Answer the question, yes or no. Is there any written policy?"

"No!"

"Thank you. That is all."

"Any redirect?" Judge Thomas asked.

"No. That was our last witness. The case for the

State rests."

The judge turned toward Harrington. "Is there any objection to recessing until tomorrow?"

"None, your honor!"

CHAPTER EIGHT

REV. BELMONT CLOSES CASE FOR D.A. TOMORROW DEFENSE WITNESSES WILL APPEAR ON THE STAND

Rev. Belmont was questioned concerning the case, and had the following to say:

"I don't see how Harrington can possibly believe he will do more than make a lot of noise. While he has made some very interesting points, so far, I don't see how he could possibly believe he'll get a ruling in favor of his client. The law is the law. It is as simple at that!"

Harrington, questioned outside the Courthouse today, said; "There is little doubt that a ruling will be made in favor of Benny, and that it will be history making—and change the whole image of *ersatzes* in general."

An authority on the subject, who requested that his name be withheld, claimed that the whole trial was a farce and that it would end up as the downfall of Harrington's reputation as a lawyer.

It is expected that Harrington will put Jeannie Brown on the stand, even though he refused to make any statement to the effect.

* * * * * * *

Jay Harrington was in his apartment, watching the media news with Ann Laymont, when the front door buzzer sounded.

He stood and went to the door which opened for him.

Mayor Sherman, a tall, thin man with nervous blue eyes, stepped into the apartment, followed by two other men.

"Well, well," Harrington cried in his best courtroom style, pressing the button which closed the door. "What do I owe this unexpected visit—"

"Harrington," Mayor Sherman said, interrupting the lawyer with a quick action of his thin right hand. "I'll come right to the point!"

Harrington held back a nasty retort. He had never gotten along with this professional politician, and didn't like the idea of the man storming into his apartment as if he owned the place. But caution warned him to play his hand close to the chest until he discovered exactly what the man was after.

"What's the point, Dan?" Harrington asked, purposely using the man's first name.

"You're to soft pedal the trial. Let this thing drop! There's been a lot of pressure—politically. I don't want you to win this case! That's an order from high up!" The man's words were choppy, his

124

finger stabbed the air with each one he spoke, as if hitting an imaginary Harrington.

For a moment the lawyer stood there, amazed. It was Ann Laymont who broke the stony silence.

"Well, Mr. Mayor—what right do you have to tell a lawyer, a professional man, independent of the City Hall, that he should or shouldn't honestly defend a client?" Her face was livid with anger as she stood there, hands on her hips, glaring at the other man.

The Mayor turned, glanced at Ann and then looked back at Harrington. "This is a farce and you know it!"

"I don't know what you're all so fired up about! After all, your representative of the DA's office seems quite sure that-"

"That's the point. We will win—but you could make it very sticky. We don't want this thing. I didn't really believe you'd put up such a fight. We felt it would be better for all concerned if you threw the case. If this...*ersatz* is given over to Brown, it could have political repercussions for years. It could change the whole texture of the social living. It can be very, very dangerous. And we don't want that. Now do you?"

Harrington sighed. "I don't see where it will make any difference one way or another. In the first place, all we're after is letting Brown keep the *ersatz*—there's nothing political about that. The issue is simple enough. The sale of personal property. That's all!"

"But," Mayor Sherman announced, "the wrong kind of ruling could cause both a political and religious explosion. It would throw things in favor of the opposition party. That wouldn't be good for my office and-"

"I think you're looking up the wrong rocket tube, Mayor. Why don't you just change your stand on this? It could turn out to be good for your political career. After all—during your term of office you were the one who was at least indirectly responsible for changing the course of history. Every mother is silently pulling for Benny—merely because it saved the life of Jeannie, a little girl. Why don't you make a public statement to that effect?"

The Mayor looked at the two men who were with him. It was a questioning, almost pleading expression.

The shorter man, stocky, with a bald head, said; "I'm the Mayor's political writer and I can assure you, Mr. Harrington, that it would be impossible to make any public statement now. What if the case turned against Benny?"

"Then you'd be able to claim an honest surprise. And then say that you really believed Benny should have been sold to Brown—but you wouldn't step in the way of justice, even though your opinion differed and—"

"And at which point," Mayor Sherman broke in, irritated, "I'm looking like a fool!"

Harrington breathed heavily for a few moments, then sighed. "I'm sorry, gentlemen, but I'm afraid you'll have to solve your political problems yourselves."

The stocky writer smiled, his eyes narrowed. "I don't think you quite understand the position the mayor is in. If he were to make a statement against the *ersatz* tonight—and then the outcome of the case favored his viewpoint, then you can see how good that would look on his record. A just man—a man who believed in what the public believed in—and...well, you can see what I'm talking about!"

"I'm sorry. Talk to your DA's office. Maybe they would be willing to throw the case," Harrington laughed.

Mayor Sherman frowned. "We could make it well worth your considering—"

"Get the hell out of here!" Harrington snapped, moving toward the door. "That's a bribe and—"

The stocky writer smiled, a careful, controlled smile. "What in the world made you think we meant that? After all, the Mayor wouldn't think of doing such a thing. We were merely talking about the—"

"Get out!" Harrington yelled.

The three men glared at him and then finally walked out of the apartment. Once they were gone, Harrington turned to Ann Laymont, his shoulders relaxed, tired.

She came up to him, slipping her arms around his neck, saying: "They must think you've won!"

Harrington laughed bitterly. "Are you kidding! They just want to play this thing for themselves to their best advantage! That's all. Belmont isn't a fool. He knows exactly what he's doing. I'm working against impossible odds. This is all a farce, like everybody says. We *are* trying to do something which should have been done a long time ago. We are proving that the *ersatzes* are something more than mere machines. It doesn't matter if Benny is turned over to Brown or not. That isn't the issue, and hasn't been—as you know. It's a point of principle—that's all. Win or lose we merely make a few

127

public statements which might, in time, change public attitudes toward the *ersatzes*."

"And that's why I love you so much!" Ann announced, kissing his lips.

They stood close to one another for a long time, Harrington finding it hard to believe what he'd just heard.

There was no question in his own mind as to how he felt about Ann Laymont, but not until then had he really been able to think she might return his love in the same way. Neither of them had a chance to say anything more about that subject, because a sudden spark burst into flame between them. Their kiss fired.

A few moments later they moved into the bedroom.

She lay down on the bed, waiting for him, and when he slid down next to her the mere feel of the woman was in itself a beauty and perfection. He wanted to hold her forever. He wanted to know the delightful contentment of merely being near the woman he loved. It amazed Harrington that this could he happening to them. He knew, for the first time, that they would be together for life—and that nothing else mattered. Later, he told her what he felt. He caressed and murmured his words of love, his inner desires and desperate passions which had been burning within him so long.

And when he was finished, Harrington realized he had said: "How about us getting married?"

She merely laughed and hugged closer: "I never thought you'd ask!"

* * * * * * *

The courtroom was hushed, waiting, expectant. The excitement which had been generated the day before seemed to hang over everybody in the room. Each person was anxiously waiting for the dramatic unexpected of which Harrington was famous.

"Call Doctor Linton to the stand," Harrington instructed in a bright, loud voice.

Linton, a tall, intelligent looking man with gray hair and dark brown eyes, was sworn, identified as a psychologist, and then sat in the witness box.

"Tell me, Dr. Linton, in your considered opinion, what is the difference between Man and animal?"

"The ability to judge right from wrong—to reason."

"And, correct me if I'm wrong, but doesn't the ability to judge right and wrong mean to be able to see some ..."

"Objection. The Counsel is leading the witness."

"Sustained."

"Then I'll ask you to tell me—by example what you would consider the ability to judge right from wrong—to reason."

"Well, I take it you wish to know if making a decision concerning a problem—or a series of events which demand certain action—is the ability to reason."

"That is correct."

"I object to the line of questioning since it is obvious that the Counsel has instructed the witness and-"

"There were no instructions," Harrington announced.

"Objection overruled. I see no reason why the doctor shouldn't come right to the point. The publicity of this *ersatz* incident has made the issue quite public."

"Continue, Dr. Linton."

"I would say that this is an example of reasoning."

"Without making any comparison of Benny with a human being—or any *ersatz* with a human being—could you please tell the Court how you would interpret his actions in saving the girl's life?"

"I would say it is an example of a subject reasoning a series of events—thinking out what possible end results might take place and then acting on its judgment."

"What would this mean? Concerning the *ersatz* named Benny."

"Simply that he has a definite ability to judge; to make a decision of action and even against its own-"

"Objection. The witness is making a conclusion on a subject of which he has no person knowledge. He has no way of knowing what was good and what was bad for the *ersatz* in question."

"You will rephrase," Judge Thomas admonished.

Harrington said: "First answer this: Would it be logical to assume that when a creature runs away that it has reasons to do so?"

"I would say so."

"Could that reason be fear?"

"It *could* be."

"Couldn't it be desire to seek freedom?"

"Objection to this line of questioning, for it calls for—"

"Calls for nothing of the kind," Harrington cut in. "But I will rephrase the question to satisfy Rev. Belmont." He turned to the witness. "In a *human* this sort of action would indicate a possible urge to survive—considering the circumstances involved in the apparent actions of Benny."

"Under those conditions there is no question—that is, assuming that the *ersatz* was running to escape death. It is the survival instinct."

Belmont stood, "He is not an expert on *ersatzes*. His opinion concerning them is out of order."

"The objection is sustained and well taken. Refrain from such statements."

Harrington sighed and asked: "Then tell me if you would consider such an action—physical action—which Benny acted out, if it were done by a human, would it indicate survival instinct?"

"Yes."

"Now tell me—do machines have survival instincts?"

"Objection. He is not an expert on machines."

"Sustained."

"Then tell me this: is there any knowledge in your science of anything other than the animal kingdom having the instinct of survival?"

"No."

"Would you say this is the difference between animal and inanimate objects?"

"Yes."

"Then considering the actions of Benny, would they seem to be very much the actions of a human being under the same conditions?"

"Objection."

"Overruled. You may answer that question."

"Yes—they are very much like a human might act."

"Then you would equate the actions as indicating something other than selfish?"

"Objection since it asks for a conclusion which the witness could not possibly have knowledge."

"Since Counsel for the defense has used the word 'indicating' I will allow the question to be asked and answered."

"Yes, it would indicate a form of selflessness."

"Therefore an act of kindness?"

"Yes."

"That is all. Thank you." Harrington sat, triumphant.

Belmont approached the witness. He glared at the man and then asked: "But tell me—you wouldn't consider the *ersatz* human?"

"That is quite obvious."

"You do admit it is a creation of man?"

"Yes."

"You do admit that it is made in a factory of synflesh and steel?"

"Yes."

"You do assume that there would be no Divine Soul?"

"Yes."

"You do admit that it is not an animal?"

"Yes."

"You do admit it is neither animal or man or anything other than a machine?"

"Objection."

Judge Thomas turned to Belmont. "The Court has already ruled on the term 'machine' concerning the *ersatz*—though we didn't realize at the time the

132

full implications of that ruling which the defense counsel quite cleverly managed to bring into issue. But considering the ruling you will have to reword your question."

"You admit it is neither man nor animal?"

"This is correct."

"Then what would you call it?"

"An *ersatz*. A device which was created for a specific purpose. A device which seems to have the ability to—"

"That is quite *enough!*" Belmont interrupted. "I'm through with this witness."

"Call Carlton Gentry MacManners to the stand," Harrington ordered.

A murmur of surprise sounded through the audience. Belmont looked at Harrington.

Harrington stood, walked forward and looked at the witness after he had been sworn in. "Could you tell the Court your background, Mr. MacManners?"

"Legal expert on *Ersatz Law*. I've written twenty texts on the subject. I have been responsible for the original development and design."

"Could you tell the Court the reasons for the law. The background?"

"The *ersatz* has built in automatic reflex action which makes it impossible for it to do harm to the human being. We don't have rules placed in the *ersatz* brain—but only an instinctive restriction against physical harm against a human. In running away, the *ersatz* Benny pushed aside his owner—without hurting him. This was not against the restriction. In saving the girl's life—it was against the self interest of the *ersatz*.

"The reason that there is a legal ruling saying

that any *ersatz* which runs away should be disposed of was in the belief that such an *ersatz* was defective, not working right, had no functional place in our society—was of no use to its owner. An *ersatz* was developed for a single purpose—without any other function in mind. We have robots to do what work man doesn't wish to do—but the government restricts their work to dangerous labor. There must be work for all, so that there is a smoothly working society. Idleness would crumble society in a matter of weeks. The *ersatz* has one function: It was believed for the mere purpose of being used as an outlet for violence and personal frustrations. Now a new viewpoint is suggested—and if the *ersatz* can perform in this way, why not? Who knows what the *ersatz* might offer in the distant future? I don't! But certainly a more sophisticated response and reaction that a mere robot, no matter how sophisticated it might be—there are limits there. The *ersatz*, on the other hand, may prove to have unlimited possibilities!"

"I object to these speculations!" Belmont stood, shaking a fist in the air. "Fantasy. Sci-fi!"

Harrington laughed: "I object to the objection!"

The judge tossed his hand in the air, saying: "I object to both of you and both of your objections, if you want to know the truth. So...please continue!"

"Well," MacManners huffed, sitting up and leaning forward slightly, a bright gleam in his eyes, "I imagine that *ersatzes* could be used in space exploration, far more sensitive to the issues involved—the human issues, that is! Robots and computers have limits, even when programmed to their ultimate state. *Ersatzes*, while some might consider

134

them nothing more than highly developed mere robots in synflesh, are somewhat different, I suppose…and here's where we get into a tough area."

"How's that?"

"Well, without suggesting something other that, this is personal speculation, it is a step between machine and animal!"

"Objected to!"

"Yes," the judge announced, "I object, too! This machine and animal debate is …"

"Sir," said Harrington, "Mr. MacManners did directly point out it was merely his…what was it? It was speculation on his part."

Belmont moaned, "Do we have to deal with all this tripe?"

The judge nodded. "It is pushing the line. We aren't dealing with science fiction, here!"

MacManners said: "It isn't sci-fi, it is personal thoughts based on long experience and scientific knowledge!"

There was a prolonged silence, then the judge banged his gavel several times, saying nothing; quite obviously offering a mere outpour of his own frustrations.

Harrington watched for several moments then nodded.

"Thank you, Mr. MacManners." Harrington walked to his bench and sat down, a pleased smile on his face.

Belmont stood, looked at the witness and then after a long hesitation, said: "You say that an *ersatz* might have other functions—but isn't this something other than the issue here before the Court? Forgetting all your fantasy bull! Aren't we actually concerned with only one thing? Benny is no different from any other *ersatz*—the Law reads clearly on the point and says that all runaway *ersatzes* are to be destroyed. Or, rather, to use a more scientific term, *malfunctioning ersatzes.*"

"That is correct," MacManners admitted.

After a short silence Belmont turned to his bench. "I'm through with the witness."

Harrington stood, saying: "Call Jeannie Brown to the stand!"

Jeannie had on a highly starched red dress. As she stepped into the witness box the judge turned and asked her: "Do you know the difference between a lie and the truth?"

"Yes," she said in a shaky voice.

"You promise to tell the truth?"

"Yes."

The judge nodded to Harrington who walked over to Jeannie, smiling in a fatherly way.

"Tell me what happened that day you met Benny."

"We talked. He was a nice man."

"Objected to!" Belmont boomed in a loud voice.

Judge Thomas looked seriously at Jeannie. "If you must call the *ersatz* something—use the name Benny."

"I'm sorry," she quickly said in a small voice, her eyes wide with alarm. "I thought he was a...man. He was nice. I liked him."

Harrington said: "Don't be afraid. Nobody's going to hurt you, Jeannie. We only want to know what happened that day. Can you remember?"

"Yes."

"Well, you talked, didn't you? I mean, Benny

136

and you talked."

"Yes."

"What did you think about Benny?"

"He was very nice. He talked and was friendly. I liked him. I want him so very much."

"What happened after he left?"

"I ran after him."

"Why?"

"I wanted to see him again."

"You liked him and wanted to see him again because he was so nice. Is that right?"

"Objected to on the grounds he is leading the witness."

Harrington turned to the judge. "She is just a child and needs help on this and—"

"I understand," Thomas said kindly, smiling at the little girl. "Under the circumstances I believe she should be led. Objection overruled."

"You liked him and wanted to see Benny again because he was so nice, was that right?"

"Yes. I think he's awful nice." Jeannie's face beamed, smiling, her puffy cheeks pink and flushed, her eyes wide with love and excitement "And you ran across the street. Benny rushed to you and picked you up and took you out of the street?"

"Yes."

"Now tell me, Jeannie, what would you do if the Court let you have Benny?"

"Oh I would play with him. I would love him. We could jump rope, play hopscotch together. All sorts of things. It would be fun."

"Would you ever hurt him?"

"Oh, *never*. I would *love* him!" Harrington turned his eyes to Belmont, smiled triumphantly and then said: "Thank you Jeannie." He sat down.

Belmont stood, looked at Jeannie, hesitated and then sat. "No cross examination."

"That rests the case for the Defense," Harrington announced.

CHAPTER NINE

"Court will listen to the summary of the learned Rev. Belmont for the State," Judge Thomas announced.

Belmont stood, reaching his full, regal height, turning his eyes toward the telecams, smiling, sure of himself, and then marched into the middle of the courtroom, faced the judge and then looked at Harrington.

"I believe that this is a simple case. I believe there is no doubt in the Court's mind as to the conclusions which the witnesses have brought forth, proven without doubt.

"While some startling statements have been made, some amazing opinions expressed that lend a strange new light on the subject of *ersatzes*—which it would be foolish not to recognize—I don't believe there was one scrap of evidence suggested or pointed out that could possibly cause the Law to look upon this matter with any thought of bending its only possible decision.

"As I said at the beginning, the Law reads very clearly on this issue. Any *ersatz* whosoever shows any faulty functioning—such as resistance, or running away—or in any way might do other than submit to the will of its human master, will be taken to the Syn-Lab and done away with.

"There is no possible evidence even suggested—that the State could, under any circumstances, accept as a reason for twisting the existing laws.

"The *ersatz* ran away. The *ersatz* willfully made a move against its master's desires. It even went so far as to touch a human being. Not once—but twice. The first time in violence. The second time in an admittedly strange action of saving a little girl's life.

"But the charges against the *ersatz* can never be wiped out. It can never be 'forgiven' for there is no such thing as forgiving a machine. Plus it would be a very slippery slope we don't wish to slide down!

"That the *ersatz* is a creation of man—and be it not a so-called machine in the strict sense of this Court's ruling, it is a synthetic device which wouldn't have been possible without the development of machines and inventions.

"To suggest—as the learned defense counsel has so done—that an *ersatz* is to be given consideration because it can do things around the house, that it can show an act of mercy, that it can reason—as he suggests, supported by twisted statements of witnesses—is outrageous.

"*Ersatzes* are *not* of a higher order than animals. That one would reward a dog or cat—or any pet—and not consider rewarding a synthetic device is *not* unnatural.

"Do you reward your washing machine?

"Do you reward your car?

"Do you reward any mechanical or synthetic device, created by man, for doing a good job? A job which it was created to do!

140

"This is outrageous!!

"It is against the Bible to even suggest that an *ersatz*—or any synthetic device—should be considered as an individual.

"An *ersatz* is an *ersatz*. Nothing more. Nothing but a functioning synthetic device created for the sole purpose of providing an outlet for human emotions and tensions. A substitute for violence.

"When one malfunctions then it should be disposed of. There is nothing malicious about this. There is nothing wrong with it; nothing sinful or degenerate. A machine made to wash dishes that doesn't wash dishes is disposed of. There is nothing emotional about this. There is nothing wrong with it. A pure simple logical conclusion.

"I see—no less strongly than before—no reason why this *ersatz* should not be disposed of.

"I don't even see why it was necessary for this whole issue to be brought up. It is unreasonable. Insane.

"The opinion and demand of the State is that the Law be carried out and the *ersatz* be done away with.

"I so move on the grounds that no evidence has even been suggested that could possibly lead to any other conclusion regarding this law.

"*There* rests the case for the State."

Belmont stomped to his bench and slammed down into the chair.

Judge Thomas turned to Harrington.

Harrington stood, but did not move from where he was.

"This case has not been brought up to twist existing Laws but to point out that they are unjust. It

141

has not been my contention to suggest that all *ersatzes* be given equal rights with humans or that we give them freedom of action and movement.

"We are concerned only about the *ersatz* named Benny.

"We believe that the evidence is conclusive. We believe that it is an obvious fact that Benny is neither malfunctioning nor imperfect. But rather that Benny—whether different from others of his kind or not—is worthy of something other than disposal. Though we do believe that Benny's actions prove beyond a doubt that *ersatzes* are more than we—their creators—intended them to be. We believe that the whole *ersatz* problem should be looked upon in a different light. We believe that Benny has showed *by his actions* that we have created a wonderful being—a being which is noble, which has a sense of values and which has a very human emotional make-up.

"Benny ran away because he wanted to survive.

"It must have been obvious to Benny that he couldn't get far, but a survival instinct pushed him into action. That—like his human creators—every instant of life was worth living—worth keeping, no matter what. He faced death in either case—but he chose to extend life as long as possible. Then, when other factors came into being, Benny chose to save the little girl's life—no matter what it cost him. He didn't think about the possible dangers involved. What he did was instinctive reflex action. The facts are simple. He *did* save the girl's life.

"Who knows what the *ersatz* is capable of doing?

"Nobody knew what electricity might do.

"Nobody knew what the New World would give—that our nation would be founded on this hemisphere.

"Many things that man has done—or created—have turned into something more glorious than intended.

"Nobody knew that atomic power would give us so much. Or that the computer would invent the Internet and all those wonders which developed from that point!

"The *ersatz* was created for one purpose—but who knows what other purposes it might be used for?

"And advanced explorer to the planets, a substitute for a human in landing on new worlds? Who knows?

"But that isn't the issue facing us right here and now!

"We are dealing with the actions of one *ersatz* by the popular name of Benny.

"There is no issue of reward—in the sense of humans giving rewards to another human—but merely a statement that there is nothing at all wrong with letting Benny continue to live—there is *everything* wrong with disposing of him.

"He is *not* different—and there is nothing wrong with him. Unless you would have us believe that saving a girl's life is wrong.

"How many humans would have tried to save her?

"There is no argument about that, because we know there are very few humans who would risk their lives A hundred years ago that was true—but today humans value their own lives—there is no reason to save another human at the risk of our own life.

"Maybe Benny proved something to us, which we had forgotten. That there is nothing more wonderful and more valuable than the human life. For he—an *ersatz*—was willing to give his in place of a little girl's.

"What more noble an act would one wish another creature to perform?

"And are we to dispose of the creation which did such a noble thing?

"And there is no harm.

"This is what Mr. MacManners pointed out. The law was placed into effect for the sole purpose of doing away with faulty *ersatzes*—not for the 'public belief' of punishing *ersatzes*.

"But there is surely nothing wrong with Benny—unless self-sacrifice is wrong.

"If that be wrong, then all our ancestors who gave their lives for civilization were wrong.

"All the past heroes are to be damned.

"All the great men in the past are to be considered criminals for they did acts of self-sacrifice.

"For that is all that Benny is guilty of.

"Unless you must consider his running away.

"But that was only the desire to live. The desire to continue to live for a few moments longer.

"Every creature on Earth can understand that emotion.

"So all that Benny is guilty of is having very human emotions and instincts. And the act of saving the life of a little girl.

"If this is what you would deprive him of his life for—then you must also deprive every human

144

who feels the same things, of his life.

"The *ersatz* is the greatest of all creations of man. The *ersatz* is the perfection of man's science and genius. And we would wish to degrade it by being blinded to this simple fact.

"The *ersatz* is a tribute to man.

"The *ersatz* is all but human.

"The *ersatz* is more than man ever thought it possible to create. The *ersatz* has every quality except the Divine Soul which only God can give.

"And for that reason I suggest, I demand, that the Court acknowledge this fact by releasing Benny so that he may be purchased by Mr. Brown."

Harrington sat down.

Judge Thomas was silent for several moments and then said: "Court will recess until tomorrow at nine. The Court Reporter will program the M-Brain on all the facts concerning this case, along with all the police statements, investigations, Syn-Lab statements and all reports and records concerning the incident—along with the recording of this trial and hearing. Tomorrow we will hear the reading on its judgment and recommendations."

After a moment Judge Thomas stood and walked from the room.

* * * * * * *

That night Jeannie Brown was unable to sleep. Across the city, in a cold room, on a large white table, Benny was lying, still unconscious, still unaware of what his actions had caused.

And in another part of the city, Edmund Canfield and Claire were lying on his large double bed, watching the Telenews.

It was a story which Edmund had written, one of a long line of articles which had slowly brought the public more and more to the side of Benny:

COURT WILL MAKE
JUDGMENT TOMORROW!

It is expected that, no matter what the judgment might be on Benny, the repercussions will be long and extensive. Even the Mayor, today, refused comment on the outcome of the trial or on his personal views. An inside story says that he would have very much liked to make public a few statements which would have been backed up by the verdict.

The emotional response to this civil trial, concerning the demand of a Citizen to be heard over a seemingly minor purchase, has outdone all the international news flashes for the last week. Mothers the world over have banded together in their hopes that Benny will be turned over to Jeannie Brown. The emotional impact of an *ersatz* saving a child's life has been fantastic.

Regardless of the outcome, it would seem only fair that Benny be turned over to Brown. An inside informant indicates that the chances are slim, in spite of the magnificent case which Harrington has presented.

146

It can only be hoped that some loophole will be discovered by the M-Brain—otherwise the case will have turned out—as Belmont stated—a big farce—which would be a terrible tragedy. And—"

Edmund Canfield flicked off the switch and turned toward Claire, letting his eyes feast on her.

She asked: "Why'd you kill the story?"

"Heard it before, somewhere…" He chuckled. Then fought down a sense of guilt. It hadn't been possible to tell her the truth about the other stories.

She studied his worried look, then smiled. "You know, Eddy me boy, I figured you did the best you could for the cause. Those stories, even in the beginning, were tainted by the sweet poison of pro-*ersatz*, even if you didn't realize it."

"What're you talking about?" He felt real alarm. This wasn't what he wanted to talk about.

"Well, you don't really think I wouldn't recognize your style?"

"Style?"

"In writing. I mean."

She looked quiet serious, then suddenly smiled. "Well, I'm not dumb. I know you did the best you could. But those stories had your touch—I knew you'd been responsible for their creation right from the start, but figured…given time you'd become convince! And I was right!"

The quick rush of joy burst up through him at her words, as she said: "You dummy! I've never known such a wonderful man!"

He merely grinned up at her for a long, lingering

moment, then said: "And you're still the most beautiful woman in the world!"

Edmund covered her lips with his own. Then he pushed away, smiling down into her eyes. "How about you marrying a hard-nosed reporter?" he asked.

Claire frowned, thought and then smiled. "You know—suddenly I realize there isn't a reason in the world why I shouldn't. I don't know a man I'd rather spend the rest of my life with. A man who will do anything for the woman he loves." She hugged closer, and he felt a wave of excitement.

How he loved this woman of his!

Then Edmund was kissing, caressing, and feeling the warm heat of her.

Like so many times in the past, when he had made love to Claire, it seemed all new, all exciting, more thrilling than with any other woman he had ever known. He knew it would last, last forever and ever. That it would last as long as he lived.

* * * * * * *

The nation waited breathlessly. Some with hope for the *ersatz* named Benny. Some with horror that he would not be disposed of. Some felt hate for the whole trial, and like the State's Counsel believed it to be a terrible farce.

The hour of nine approached and the media, which had presented experts discussing what the ethics and facts of the *ersatz* trial were all about and how they felt it should end, finally stopped and all channels turned to the Courtroom.

Judge Thomas stepped into the Court. Everything was hushed quiet as he took his place. The lines around his eyes, dark and shadowed, revealed the short sleep the night had brought him.

His voice was tired sounding as he said: "We are gathered here today to make a final judgment on the case of the State vs. Brown.

"First we will hear the decision and recommendations of the Master Court Brain on the trial and evidence, after which the Court will make its final judgment.

"Will the Court Reporter read the statement of the M-Brain."

The Court Reporter stood, a small vidcell clutched in his hands. He turned and faced the judge.

"The state of *ersatzes* is unquestionable in terms of the Law," the man read. "The statements of the witness, the records of the Court, can come to only one conclusion: The Law is wrong. Still there is no loophole in this Law. While the *ersatz*'s actions call for more than what the Law states, *as now written,* to conform to the Law, there is no other action than to dispose of the *ersatz*.

"However, considering that the function of the Law is to be just and considering that the Law was written under the assumption that *ersatzes* were machines, and since this is not, necessarily always the case, it is recommended that the *ersatz* named Benny be considered separate from other *ersatzes*.

"Therefore, it would be the recommendation to allow the Law to be ignored in the case of Brown vs. State, except that such an action should be taken only on the assumption that Benny is different from other *ersatzes*—which, from expert testimony, has been proven otherwise.

"However, as the Law now stands there can be no possible choice except to follow its written statement."

The audience murmured, some sounds of agreement voicing over the general noise of protests.

Judge Thomas demanded silence and after a long time, slowly began speaking.

"The Court has listened to the pleas of both Counsels, listened to the statements of the witnesses, and now is ready to consider the recommendations of the M-Brain."

There was a moment of silence as Judge Thomas paused. Then he continued in a stronger and surer voice. "As I have already stated, the publicity which this trial has been given and the attitude of the general public will not be considered in the Court's judgment. Nor will the political pressures which have been crammed down our throats, directly and indirectly, I must admit!

"While at first I quite honestly wanted nothing to do with the case, I am now quite glad to have become a part of such an historical event.

"It is not easy to pass judgment. But putting it off will not make the task easier.

"In considering the recommendations of the M-Brain, and having listened to all that has happened in this case, it is the considered opinion that there is nothing wrong with looking upon the *ersatz* Benny as an individual example of an *ersatz*.

"While *ersatzes* were developed for the sole purpose of serving man as the master decreed, it is also just to consider the fact that *ersatzes* might possibly be more than we had planned.

"At least the *ersatz* named Benny.

"As Counsel for the Defense pointed out, Benny is guilty of only two things—fear and the. saving of a little girl's life.

"Fear, all creatures of thought will feel—all creatures of instinct will feel. The element of saving another life at the sacrifice of one's own freedom and life is something which was a part of human-ity—and should still be a part of humanity.

"There is no question in the Court's mind that Benny—without considering any comparison with any other *ersatz*—deserves more than automatic disposal. There is nothing to gain by disposing of Benny. There is everything to gain by turning him over to a family which will find use for him.

"A machine is created to be useful—not merely to perform a limited function.

"*Ersatzes,* while more than machines, were a mechanical device which turned out to be more than the creator meant them to be.

"Benny is more than we meant him to be.

"Therefore the ruling of the Court is that Benny is to be turned over to Mr. Ken Brown.

"Court dismissed."

EPILOG

The rest is historically recorded elsewhere. The events reported above, possibly authored by Claire and Edmund Canfield's son, Daniel, as some authorities suspect, certainly offer an insight into what followed a couple of decades later. The Revolution came after the natural bonding between Jean & Benny, for they were the forerunners of what soon followed.

FREE worked, as every student of history knows, and helped to create the world that now exists.

Nothing is perfect, but population control is a concern of historians, for the moral grounding of limited birth has become a part of our culture. We look into the future through the eyes of planned, intelligent expansion. Not only of Earth and the limited colonies on our solar system, but the promise of the universe as a natural, unlimited breeding ground for humanity! The Biblical pronouncements to multiply may soon, once again, be in favor—but within an endless landscape! Until then we are all willing to await the fulfillment of our natural dreams of human expansion.

The future, which could not be even guessed at by the people living back then, now promises us exploration of interstellar space in full partnership with our brothers:

The *Ersatzes*!

They have now become our first explorers across the distance between the stars, and are able to adapt to almost any possible alien environment existing. The first starships are already beginning to return with the exciting news of future worlds to explore.

The *ersatzes* have become a blessing to Mankind's past, present and future!

THE TALISMAN

THE TALISMAN

Even if we had remembered the old saying about Greeks bearing gifts, most of us couldn't have resisted the sales pitch.

I should have been more suspicious, having come from the big city. We'd moved to Dales, a small farming town, when I was a little past fifty—some ten years ago. I'd come for my health—which was in bad shape—though I didn't expect a magically prolonged and vigorous life, only a few extra years. If we're lucky we survive into our seventies and might even get into our eighties and be thankful for the extra years. Heck, these days, with the advanced medical discoveries, many of us are going into our nineties. But I'm a realistic sort, and a medical doctor; not a believer in Voodoo.

Yet what followed Mr. Smith's visit seemed nothing short of witchcraft; him and his damnable Talisman. It was the event of Ms. Black's baby that sent silent shock waves through the county. But that comes later.

It all started with Mr. Smith. He was small and only a bit aggressive. Those compelling dark eyes were anxious to grab you.

The instant I realized he was a salesman I started to close the door in his face.

He lifted a small hand, the lines etched deeply into his palm, fingers almost gnarled, bony, the skin discolored, off-white. "Please! It is so important to both of us that you listen."

There was something haunting about the desperate quality of his plea, as if the very existence of our lives depended on my cooperation. That stopped me from slamming the door shut.

His gaunt frame looked terribly frail; those dark eyes had the impelling stare of a small desperate puppy.

"Who's there?" Mildred called from the kitchen. The aroma of home cooked baked cherry pie was just beginning to drift through the house, mixed with the spicy promise of beef stew. The man had a nerve invading our privacy on the one day of the week we were normally able to rest. The people in Dales County used to be tightly religious, and believed it was a sin even to be ill on the Holy day. *Nobody* was supposed to work on Sunday; not even a doctor.

But Mr. Smith pushed into the house.

Mildred came from the kitchen, flowery apron about her ample waist, hair pinned back into a tight ponytail. A friendly smile broke instantly from her wide lips. Mildred seldom turned away strangers. "Hello. What can we do for you?"

"It is what we can do for one another," the man's skinny lips announced around a tight grin. "You're Mildred Henderson Shelby Benson, of course...right?"

"How in the world did you know?" She was taken by surprised. Even her best friends didn't know her full name.

He turned to me. "Dr. Glenn Thomas Benson. A specialist in childcare who was childless himself. You've been a GP since you came here to Dales."

This should have warned me. But of what?

"By way of explanation." He quickly stepped across the small living room, taking a seat on our overstuffed chair. He leaned intently forward. "By the way of explanation, a good salesman does his homework. Just let me make my pitch and I'll go."

Those eyes again, pleading, yet so compelling, drilled into ours, flitting back and forth between us.

"Please be comfortable. Sit while I do my pitch." It sounded so innocent, and yet was such a command. We sat next to one another on the battered pink sofa. Mildred grabbed my hand.

I noticed the black bag he was holding on his lap. I hadn't seen it before.

"Now, it is my job to convince you to believe that you can't live without what I have to offer." He glanced down at the black bag on his lap. "Of course, all salesmen must convince their prospects to need something they don't want."

Mildred's fingers were hot and damp, trembling, as they squeezed mine.

"I won't claim I'm working my way through college. I'm a bit old for that line, now don't you think?" His grin was almost icy. "I won't use any silly excuse like most salesmen do to shove something down people's throats. Nothing but honesty is my approach. Such a direct approach should be worth at least a few minutes of your time."

Mildred's lips hung open, soundlessly. I merely shrugged, wishing he would leave.

As if reading my thoughts, he said: "Of course,

you're anxious to consume the delicious food the Missus here fixed. I'll take only a few moments."

Flexible fingers, almost rubbery, boneless, slipped over the clasp of the tiny black bag. "Now, let me warn you, from the first, this is something few people would think of needing...yet you must have one."

One gnarled hand reached deeply into the small bag, wrist disappeared, and then forearm. It was as if he were reaching into some bottomless pit.

"You must be wondering why you should be willing to take something you don't need or want. Well, observe!"

He made a dramatic movement of his arm, lifting it out of the tiny black bag. With a flourish he presented a furry pink powder-puff.

"This is it!" He placed the object on the coffee table before us. It rested there quietly, doing exactly nothing. For a moment the man merely sat there gazing at us, eyes fanatically watching for any reaction.

I finally managed: "What...is it?"

"Oh, of course, I forgot. A Talisman." He let the statement sink into our minds like a feather attempting to penetrate thick oil.

"So?" Mildred asked in a small voice. "What?"

"A Talisman. Brings you luck, you know. Has magical properties. Does wonders. He paused just a moment. Then added, with a playful wink: "Might even put you out of business, give you the retirement you've always wanted!

He smiled quite generously.

"Come on, Mr. Smith, what's the gag?" I demanded, a bit angrily. "You're taking up our Sunday afternoon—"

"Please. This is serious! With my Talisman you'll be safe from all harm, from loss of life...even acts of Gods...you'll remain happy and secure and safe...have a long life...what else is a Talisman for? In primitive times it was assumed to have magical powers. It brought luck. Observe this one."

He made a quick motion over the puff, fingers lightly touching it. At that instant it seemed to move, perhaps from the action of his fingers making contact with it. One could not believe otherwise. It swelled as if taking a deep breath, and turned a deeper crimson. But nothing more.

"See? Very responsive. Stroking it will bring you luck. That's all you have to do. Everyday stroke it. Nothing more. It will always look after you, see that no harm comes your way; protect you both from all evil influences." Then leaning a little closer, eyes intense as they shifted from me to Mildred, he said a bit too casually: "You can never tell what tomorrow will bring. This Talisman is yours to keep, for life. Just ask...and it will protect you from harm..." He broke off, grinned, said: "Well, let's just say you'll be happy as long as you stroke it once a day, each and every day."

My impulse was to take the man by the arm and lift him bodily out of the house. "Mr. Smith, you must be kidding...in this day and—"

"I'm quite serious. Please...I'm merely attempting to offer you continued happiness until the day you die. Is that a crime?"

"I've heard enough rot. I'm not interested in buying—"

"Please. You misunderstand. It is *free*! No

strings. Just keep it. Stroke it. And I promise that no harm will ever come to you until the day you die of old age—very old age, beyond the normal three, four or more score and—"

I fell back on the sofa, unable to speak. There was that compelling command in his eyes. I didn't hear all of what he said for some moments, but picked up the thread as he stated:

"My company's doing an experiment. We're trying to prove that there's nothing to the old story about people refusing free gold bricks. Though, of course, we aren't offering gold bricks, but the point is the same. Our company hopes that people just might accept a Talisman. What harm? Let me leave this one with you. I promise if you merely touch it each day, you will live a very long life. Your future is assured."

He was standing now, closing the bag, still gazing intently into our eyes.

"But—" I said, standing. "I don't believe there isn't—"

"Oh, a catch?" He turned, and then stared towards the sofa. "Then, of course, that's a totally different matter. I *could* sell you some objects, but you'd find them quite useless. If you won't accept a gift from a stranger...well, then, let me see..." He studied me very carefully, and then glanced at Mildred. "How about twenty dollars. Would that seem fair to you?"

My wife gasped.

I turned to see Mildred leaning over the coffee table, index finger pressed against the little puff. The Talisman seemed to pulse, become very deep pink where her flesh touched it. Shadow? Illusion?

She gasped again.

The expression on Mildred's face was almost ecstatic. She looked beautiful, deep blue eyes gazing up into mine, pleading. For a moment I actually had the illusion that she was much younger again, like my bride of many years ago.

I started to say something, but instead found myself reaching towards the Talisman.

"Touch it, darling..." Mildred urged.

My first impulse was to grab the damned thing, throw it at Mr. Smith, and shove him out of our house. Instead, I extended an index finger. On contact the thing reacted with what seemed a pleased gasp. It felt almost alive, a furry, very soft, slightly cool creature. It deepened in color. Nothing more happened. Though I did experience a strange personal sensation of sudden well-being. That was surely a relief—nothing more.

I mean, I hadn't turned to stone or anything like that upon contact with the little puff.

I turned to face Mr. Smith.

The man had disappeared.

I glanced at Mildred. "Where?"

She shrugged, but didn't seem concerned. She simply said: "He left the darling Talisman..."

I went to the door. The street was empty. The man had totally vanished.

As I returned to the house, Mildred said: "Strange little man. Such an odd thing, leaving it...think he really meant to collect the money?"

I shrugged, suggesting we forget the whole matter and have dinner. I could throw the Talisman out later. Of course, I didn't.

I forgot all about the man and the puff until the

next morning when, while walking through the living room, I stopped by the table where the Talisman lay. I absent-mindedly ran my fingertips across the furry back. That strange sense of well being surged through me.

The story about Smith raged around town. It seemed he had talked to everybody in our community that Sunday afternoon. Or perhaps there were several Mr. Smiths. One of the odd things is that we all accepted such oddities without too much question. I mean, if you approached it logically, here he was all over the place in just about the same time, with everybody. Nobody could have moved that fast, been everywhere at once, unless he was more than one. That didn't make sense, of course, but for some reason we all simply fluffed over the illogical logic and said silently to ourselves, I suppose: Well, there must have been more of him. So big deal!

Old Man Johnson said: "1 threw the bum out! I ain't gonna have nothin' to do with no Talisman or such. Work of the Devil, if you ask me!"

Carl Larson, owner of the General Store, offered: "I think the Talisman's okay. Wish I could've sold it at the store." Commercial SOB. But a nice one. Dear man, did favors for everybody in town from time to time.

Most couples accepted the gift. A bit mystified; but beyond that, they considered the whole thing an odd commercial "gag"—nothing more. A few people had actually paid the $20.

Those who had the Talisman automatically touched it every morning. It was a ritual. The fluffy thing always "sighed" as if in thanks.

Oddly enough, Reverend Smiles, who seldom

had smiled, was less harsh than some disapproving members of his church. "I certainly don't believe it has anything to do with Satan. Doesn't have the mark of *the* Devil. Though, of course, I didn't take one. The Good book is all anyone truly needs for protection from all evil spirits and such. I'd say the little puff is harmless enough."

So much for the value of a Godman's words!

Rev. Smiles was found in his car, dead, a few days later.

What followed stunned all of us. He was just the first to go.

Almost immediately the other fatal accidents took place. Old Man Johnson had burned up in bed; a smoking accident. A car slid over a muddy road, overturning, killing Al Kelly and his family; lightening struck down a couple as they walked in the woods; a barn folded in on its owners. A gas stove exploded. Homes were burned down—no known explanation. The most unusual thing about these accidents was that they took place within the following month; a collective mass killing for so small a community.

There was some serious interest from the authorities concerning the deaths, State Police and all that. Even had a man from the city paper doing a bit of investigating around the county. It all caused quite a stir.

A headline story was written that made a short ripple in our community and then was forgotten as other things caught our attention.

MULTI-DEATHS PLAGUE DALE COUNTY

The mass fatal accidents have been completely investigated by the authorities and though they happened over a very short span of time are not considered anything more than a serious of concurrent and unrelated tragedies. As one authority stated: "There's no accounting for such events; probably doesn't happen like that in a thousand years. But there is every reason to consider it being a dreadful oddity.

I was quoted at the bottom of the article as the "local doctor" having said: "What else other than coincidence could have caused the accidents?"

It was Ms. Black, the town's Old Maid, who pointed out the obvious to us. After her cousins the Goodwins were found dead in their bedrooms, cause unknown, she said: "Haven't you noticed? *Everybody who didn't take a Talisman has now died!*"

Maybe the rest of us were just too busy living and doing our bit for the community to have noticed. I didn't take it too seriously, though. I merely said: "You aren't suggesting there's a connection..."

Her crinkled old face spread into a road map of lines. "I'm saying that everybody who didn't take a Talisman has died. That's all I've said. I think the Talisman is a Magical charm. And it protects us from harm. Them that didn't take it...were killed!"

I frowned, uncertain as to what to say. "Come on, now, you can't be serious. What you're suggesting is…a bit silly. And dangerous, too. If people started believing such…stuff…"

"I'm suggesting the Talisman is what it was claimed to be. I think we're alive because we took one! You just see if I'm not right! Check it out if you don't believe me! Those who mocked the Talisman are dead—those who took one and loved it are still alive!"

It didn't take much checking in such a small, tight community. Though people were reluctant to talk about the Talisman. The media people and the authorities had missed the connection. Of course, there was no reason for them to consider the Talisman—it was, in a way, our town secret. Outsiders didn't notice the little puff as being significant. It was ignored. Even we didn't make any connection. But the fact was: Ms. Black was right! Only those people who had not taken a Talisman had met with fatal accidents. Even then, this hardly seemed all conclusive, although just as suddenly as they had started the accidents stopped—and nobody else died.

Still, who wanted to rock the boat? For whatever reason, nobody was willing to take it out on the Talisman. Who would dare? What if the Talisman really did have some kind of magical powers?

The Goodwins were the last ones to have a fatal accident—Nobody even died of ill health. Nobody said anything about it. I don't know how many guessed what was happening. There was a loud silence throughout the community for a very long time, as if everybody—including Ms. Black—was too frightened to bring the subject of the Talisman up in conversation.

It is strange how people will move through life in a kind of a blind daze, allowing the impossible to seem okay, and ignoring anything that complicated their lives beyond their ability to cope. They had other matters to deal with; daily routines, survival. Just your normal, mundane exercises in living.

As a doctor, I was in a position to learn the truth through direct observation. A lot more changes were now taking place that any imaginative mind could have easily connected with the Talisman.

What might be called "side-effects" became evident within a very short time after the fatal accidents. I noticed it first in a very personal manner. My blood pressure dropped to a perfect 120 over 80. My heart murmur disappeared. More Importantly I felt stronger, was able to take longer walks almost every day through the countryside, while experiencing a fantastic emotional high. In fact, in checking out all of my body systems I noted that dramatic changes were taking place. More to the point, our romantic life gained unexpected zest—and I was acting like a man in his twenties! Mildred revealed the same kind of physical changes in her health and energy level. In the following months I began to notice similar results in all the other people in our community.

It was, again, Ms. Black, who on her six-month check up said: "I've never felt better in my life! And I know what is the cause of it all!"

Her sharp, wise eyes narrowed slightly as they looked up into mine. "You know, too, don't you, Doc?"

I started to deny my own uneasy suspicions, then said: "I'm not certain...of anything."

"Certain, pooh! What's to be certain about? We're all charmed. We're all being protected. We're all—"

"What? Fattened by the evil old witch of the west?"

"Tut-tut, Doc!" she laughed a bit sprightly. "I do believe you're mocking an old lady."

"Hardly," I said, making a quick note on her medical record. "You're quite a healthy woman— you have better health than a woman in her forties."

"And I'm the only healthy person around?" she offered, a bit pointedly.

I wanted to avoid her eyes, wasn't able to.

"Good Doctor Benson, there's a mystery here, but it has nothing to do with Witches or Demons. And you know exactly what I mean. Our mutual friend Mr. Smith appears in our town, in our community, all in one Sunday afternoon, offering his Talisman—and after that everybody who didn't take one dies. Every one else keeps their Talisman, stroking it religiously. We don't even bother with church anymore. The Talisman has become our new religious believe! And it has offered health to all of us, a kind of eternal youth! Now, tell me, how do you account for all that?'

"I don't try."

"Nor does anybody else in this county. But I've been doing a lot of thinking. And I think—"

"It is something supernatural, right?" I chuckled a bit nervously.

"Not necessarily. Not necessarily at all!" She looked very mysteriously at me, winked playfully, and then added: "There must have been several Mr. Smiths in town that day. No *one* Smith could have made all the rounds like he did. Strange, don't you think? What were all these Mr. Smiths? Did they all look alike? Sounds to me like they did, from what I've had people tell me! I've poked around. I have. Just an old busybody. Woman my age, almost eighty—well, okay, a bit past...anyway, I just sit around and I think and I figure there's something very strange going on. Not that I'm afraid, pray tell. Just an interesting pastime for an old hag like myself." She laughed at that, then said: "Anyway, I think we're being invaded!"

"By what?" I laughed, relieved, realizing the old woman was getting a bit dotty in the head.

"By Talisman, of course! Creatures from another world." She leaned close, then added, "or maybe from the place of the Devil!"

The funny thing is that I found either theory equally unsettling—and almost equally acceptable. I certainly couldn't come up with anything better, other than ignoring everything that was happening as mere coincidence. What bothered me most is that I found it just as difficult to accept coincidence as an explanation. Something was happening, but what?

Ms. Black might have been a healthy woman, a bit crazy in the head, but also the only one willing to talk about the Talisman. Nobody talked about such matters, but it was quite obvious from the expressions on their faces they were enjoying a far more vigorous life in every possible way. They were all stunningly healthy.

And like Ms. Black had stated, since Rev. Smiles had died, church had closed down. If I'd been more religious, more superstitious, perhaps I

170

would have embraced the Devil theory. It was seductive to believe that Mr. Smith had been connected with some evil demon. Somehow that idea
seemed more acceptable than any other possibility.
Finally, though, I simply had to laugh at all my silly
speculation, and went about my business. After all, I
was a scientist—and realized we were all imagining
things.

By the end of the year another fact became obvious: The Talisman was growing. Not much. Just a
very little—enough to measure.

Again it was Ms. Black who was willing to
point this fact out. She lived in a two-story wood-
frame house, and kept the Talisman in her bedroom,
on a nightstand.

"Is yours getting bigger, too?" she asked, a bit
directly.

I merely nodded, and tried to avoid the subject.
But I started making a point to note other Talisman
throughout the town and though nothing was said,
managed to observe the slow growth taking place in
these otherwise unmoving puffs of living...what? It
was obvious that everybody was aware of the
growth. Regardless, or perhaps because of this, the
owners religiously caressed the small puffs each
morning, more and more convinced that this was the
only safeguard for continued happiness.

Talk about superstitious rot! And I was buying
into it, too. Well, actually, not believing, but it was
pleasant to touch the … thing. After all, logic and
reason kept telling me it was nothing more than a
strange little puff of furry cloth; odd, but certainly
not an alien thing from outer space. Give me a
break!

But the rumors kept surfacing. A little here and a little there. As if we couldn't completely ignore reality while letting our minds continue to wallow in fantasy. To believe nothing strange was involved would be insane. And pure blindness. Or, like I said, our daily focus was more on just living from moment to moment. Actually the puff and all that was connected with it remained for the most part as background. Yet the rumors and comments surfaced to pepper our otherwise mundane lives.

Carl Larson said one morning in his store, "I'm convinced there's something to what Ms. Black claims..."

Benny Sherman, who runs the paper, said: "She's just a crazy old lady. Right, Doc?"

I shrugged that off, but asked: "What do you think?"

There were several others in the store, and they closed in around the counter where we were standing.

Benny offered: "Creatures from the Black Lagoon?"

Carl shook his head angrily. "Mock me if you want! But I'm just about convinced the Talisman is our Magic Charm!"

Vera Wellington piped in; "If you ask me, I really don't care! Why should we bother about what it is or isn't? What difference does it make? You men try to build a mountain out of a molehill! The Talisman is cute! That's good enough for me!"

Benny shrugged that away, offering: "Monsters from space, to inter-dimensional creatures, Devils and demons, or simply a childish little toy for some superstitious farmers—or magic charms, all the same to me."

Carl frowned a bit angrily, I thought, glaring at me. "Well, Doc, you haven't said what you think!"

"I try not to bother my mind with idle speculation. To be truthful...nothing going on that can't be explained away as mere coincidence. So...that's where I stand." It was almost the truth. Actually I was afraid to say more. I didn't even like to think about anything beyond that. I was consciously ignoring the fact that the puffs seemed to be growing, as if they were some kind of biological creature.

Vera statement drew general approval. "I feel better, more healthy since I've had mine! It gives me...happiness. I'll not bother with why it works. It just works! That's good enough!"

Carl agreed and added: "Damned if I'd not be willing to stroke it until Hell freezes over."

And that was the closest thing to a conversation I had with anybody in Dales about the Talisman—other than Ms. Black. Everybody just wanted to accept it blindly, with an almost religious dedication. After all, the puffs were a positive in our lives. Leave it be!

But even I found it difficult to fight down a sense of growing uneasiness. I was actually becoming superstitious. I tried to laugh it off. I knew the stroking ritual was silly. I knew the fatal accidents were explainable, too. Somehow. Beyond that point I couldn't speculate. Didn't dare!

It was in this state of suspended belief that we continued to live. Five years passed and we all refused to deal directly with the issue of the Talisman. Everybody who accepted the Talisman had watched it double in size, and we had all, until a couple of months ago, been healthy and alive. I had almost run out of work—doing little more than doctoring animals, and giving physical checkups that become more and more routine until one day I was stunned by Ms. Black coming to in to my house with an actual complaint.

She said: "I'm feeling sorta tired lately."

I examined her and found she seemed in pretty good condition, though her blood pressure had gone up some. I gave her the necessary medication. The next week I dropped over to her house. She was very pale, drawn. She met me at the door wearing a morning robe.

"Quite frankly," she stated, when I asked how she felt, "I'm getting worse. I don't know what's wrong. Even my Talisman seems strange to *me.*" She kinda laughed at that. "But then, everything *seems* strange. I'm getting old, at last. Well past eighty-five."

The expression on my face must have revealed my doubt concerning that number.

"Bragging?" I teased, directing her upstairs to her bedroom.

"Oh, no! Not that." She stumbled a few steps up the stairs, then added: "But so I'm a bit older. I'll admit that. Hell, when a gal turns fifty she wonders. She's still okay. Maybe in her prime. But by sixty…things change. Don't you know? And the age is dripping away at your flesh, bones. But at seventy you are getting to the point where you just aren't a young kid. You're what most people think of as old. By eighty, that's ancient. I simply won't admit to being…anything different. I mean…well…beyond that. Like they say: a gentleman doesn't ask a lady her age. Even if she's past her eighty decade!"

"Embarrassed? Shy? Mysterious?" I offered with a flash of a grin.

"No! Proud! To be truthful. But...to be frank I don't rightly know how old for certain. I stopped counting some time back, of course. That's for sure. You get to the point where you don't want no more birthdays and simply ignore them as fast as they come flashing by! And I don't remember the year I as born. I simply won't remember that! But my body doesn't feel right. That much I can tell you. I kinda stagger, too. Something new. I don't like that!"

Suddenly all the theories about the Talisman protecting us, offering a kind of immortality, seemed to shatter. I felt almost a perverse sense of relief.

She said, as we went into her bedroom: "Take a look at my pet Talisman...it is growing terribly big! Isn't it?"

I looked at her bed stand. The Talisman did look grossly larger than I remembered, and a very deep red in color. Almost as if it were embarrassed

I said nothing and gave her a full examination. Before I left, though, she asked, "Am I going mad? Tell me, Doc. Is my Talisman changing?"

I laughed a bit nervously. "They're always changing some, now aren't they?"

She nodded, tight-lipped. "I guess so. But I have this feeling, Doc. I remember how Mr. Smith said we'd have eighty or more plus years of good health, remember that?"

I nodded.

"And I have had that, now haven't I?" She

shrugged. "Okay past my nineties…maybe…"

I assured her she had, and probably would continue to.

"Maybe the promise has been kept for me…and I'm dying."

I tried to scoff at that. "Now why would you say such a thing?

"Just how it all adds up, if you ask me. Maybe our Mr. Smith was from the Man upstairs? Or from the man below. Or from someplace else."

"Someplace else?"

"Sure, why not? We're living in the space age. Cablevision and all that! The TV is just filled with all that spacey stuff. Them there scientist folk are talking about travel to other worlds and of alien beings on other planets. To other stars, from other galaxies."

"You've been watching too much television!" I scolded.

"I've been watching…a lot more than television! And I kinda think you almost believe me!" She winked, smiling.

"I believe you are a bit mad, to get quite blunt about it!" I stated a bit too honestly.

"Maybe. Maybe. But I see what I've seen. And I tell you I don't have much more time. Mr. Smith made his promises—and they've been kept. Good health, and my four score plus years…what more could a woman my age want? I've had a good life. And the last years have been the best! So, there!"

"But why would…Mr. Smith want to—" I broke off as she shook her head from side to side.

"If you can answer that one then you'd understand everything that happened since the Talisman

176

arrived. But you won't believe in the supernatural and you won't accept any thought of alien creatures from another world and—"

"Okay, okay," I kidded, throwing my hands up in the air. "I believe. I believe, if you want me to. But you just get well—and we can talk about it all then."

"And you won't change my mind none about it, either," she stated with finality. "The Talisman is the work of the Devil, or a gift from Heaven, or from another place or..."

"And motive?" I couldn't help asking. "Explain why."

"Motive be damned!"

"Well, now, since you've settled all that, you just take it easy from now on. And you'll be just fine," I assured her.

"I don't think so," was her stubborn reply. "I do kinda think I've had my full run."

It was the last time I saw her alive. She was never, though, in much pain. Henny Jones, who had been checking in on her, called me over to her home. He found her in bed, dead. I was pulling the sheet over her body when I heard a sound coming from across the hall.

A cold chill rushed over me. She had no pets. My eyes went to the nightstand. The Talisman wasn't there. I don't know what terrified me about that, but I felt unreasonable fear choke in around my throat.

I quickly crossed the hall, entering the dimly lit sewing room. It took a few seconds to discover where the sound was coming from. There, just in front of the sewing basket, a sad cry moaned. I almost immediately saw the small naked baby, features shriveled like all newborns, a strange wide-eyed, haunting, anguished expression in its deep black eyes. It looked pointedly in my direction.

The intense gaze unnerved me. I seemed to feel a tugging at the base of my brain, at the very center of my thought, a quick, pulsing terror.

Ms Black was an old maid, in every meaning of the word! She didn't have a lover. Even if she had, it was out of the question to consider that she could have given birth to a child. And concealing any such pregnancy from the only doctor around was impossible. But where had it come from? Whatever the explanation for the newborn baby lying there, it had to be logical.

But whose logic? I wondered, picking up the infant.

Was it some kind of monster, some being from another world? Did it have something to do with the Talisman?

I wanted to put the baby down, but couldn't. I was suddenly searching through the house, everywhere, clutching the child tightly to me.

1 did not find Ms. Black's Talisman. I did find a blanket to wrap the baby in. Even while doing all this I kept feeling an irrational impulse to smash the baby's head against the wall, as if it were some kind of terrible alien creature that must be killed. And at the same time felt an overwhelming surge to protect it from any and all harm.

I looked into the child's eyes. It was so helpless, looking up at me with such longingly jet-black eyes, so much like Mr. Smith's. Such a sight would peak the protective instincts of a demon dragon from the very depths of Hell.

"Where'd you come from?" I muttered, desperately needing to hear a human voice. "Where?"

I was already thinking: *It doesn't matter where you came from. You're a baby...we never had one of our own.*

It wasn't a rational thought. But I didn't have time to think things out. Suddenly the smell of smoke turned my attention to another danger.

Everything blurred, then. I moved automatically through a kind of vague fiery hell. Nothing made much sense—nor did I expect to find acceptable answers.

Suddenly I was out on the street. I saw the house become totally enveloped in violent flame. It was an old wood-framed building. The white-hot fire turned at the edges into a strange blue-green, consuming the building in seconds. Then it flashed out of existence, touching none of the vegetation that had surrounded the house.

I could hardly believe my senses.

The baby drew my attention back to its bundled form. It was very softly cooing. Those eyes, now so cool black, gazed powerfully up into mine.

A thought leaped at me: *The promise was kept; she lived to be near 100! And had been happy!*

It "felt" as if the baby had telepathed that message right into my brain! A shiver surged through me as I rushed home. Milly said nothing after I explained what had happened. She never asked any questions concerning the child. Nobody in the community offered any questions, either, when we kept the child.

They aren't all that sophisticated around here,

but television has made its inroads. Even Ms. Black's theories began to almost sound reasonable. For several months I was still able to hold on to my weakening argument that it could all be explained by coincidence. Then a very logical, though a bit fantastic, theory began to form in my mind.

Consider: What better way for an alien species to invade a new planet that was already overpopulated by its own intelligent life forms? Such beings would need to be protected, even nourishment— even loved. Perhaps the Talisman is some kind of embryo that needs to feed on the life-force of animal life. Does the embryo turn into what looks, acts and seems to be a human baby upon our death at old age?

I wanted to totally reject such an idea as being impossible. I kept finding ways to avoid believing we've been invaded by alien beings from another world or dimension. But I kept remembering the thought that was thrust into my mind outside Ms. Black's home: *The promise was kept. She lived to be near 100! And had been happy!*

Then a short time ago something happened that left no more room for disbelief.

Mr. Winters died at 103. The Talisman was missing; a baby was there in the house. His wife got out with the child just in time to escape the fire that burned their home to the ground.

We all wait for the next death and child. A home is being built to raise the children in one place, together.

It doesn't matter where the Talisman originated, or what the children really are. What difference does it really make? Not one of us is wiling to do anything to change matters.

After all, we are assured of as much as 100 vigorous years. None of us want to lose that. We know that to kill our Talisman would be to kill ourselves. Everybody clings and lingers to life. At all cost! And here we had a promise that was kept! Why should we give that up?

And the children are really so lovely, intelligent and deeply affectionate.

Who could turn down that kind of a deal?

ABOUT THE AUTHOR

Charles Nuetzel was born in San Francisco in 1934, and writes:

"As long as I can remember I wanted to be a writer. It was a dream I never thought would materialize. But with the help of Forrest J Ackerman, who became my agent, I managed to finally make it into print.

"I was lucky enough not only in selling my work to publishers but also ending up packaging books for some of them, and finally becoming a 'publisher' much like those who had bought my first novels. From there it as a simple leap to editing not only a sci-fi anthology, but a line of sci-fi books for Powell Sci-Fi back in the 1960s. Throughout these active professional years I had the chance to design some covers and do graphic cover layouts for pocket books & magazines."

Much of his work in covers and graphics are a result of having had a father who was a professional commercial artist, and who did a number of covers for sci-fi magazines in the 1950s and later for pocket books—even for some of Mr. Nuetzel's books.

In retirement he has become involved in swing

dancing, a long time lover of Big Band jazz. But more interestingly world travels have taken him (and his wife Brigitte) across the world, to Hawaii, Caribbean, Mexico, Kenya, Egypt, Peru, having a life-long interest in ancient civilizations. His website is full of thousands of pictures taken during these trips.